BUSHWHACKING THE BUSHWHACKERS

Suddenly the silence was shattered by a loud grating thud as Sellers's booted foot crashed into the door. Longarm could not see the man who came in, but the muzzle flashes of his revolver lighted the room like lightning bolts, and the sound of the two shots that he got off filled the air with noise and powder smoke before the would-be killer realized that the bed was empty.

Now it was Longarm's turn to kick aside the door that had shielded him. As fast as the hired gunman reacted in recovering from his first surprise, he could not bring up the muzzle of his revolver quickly enough.

Longarm triggered his Colt twice, and both slugs went home. Sellers spun around, his frame jerking at the impact of Longarm's lead. His gun barked, and in his dying reflex the gunman got off a second shot. . . .

TABOR EVANS

LONGARM

AND THE REBEL KILLERS

JOVE BOOKS, NEW YORK

LONGARM AND THE REBEL KILLERS

A Jove Book / published by arrangement with
the author

PRINTING HISTORY
Jove edition / September 1989

ISBN: 0-515-10130-3

Chapter 1

"They must have stopped there," Sha-Wo told Longarm.
As the Ponca spoke, he was gesturing to call Longarm's
attention to the blocky form of a little adobe house that
broke the flat line of the horizon ahead and was outlined
against the sunset-reddened sky. Though the hut was still
so far away that there was no chance of his words carrying
to it, Sha-Wo kept his voice low.

"Sure," Longarm agreed. Like Sha-Wo, he spoke softly
as he went on, "They'd want to stop before dark, and this
is about the only place hereabouts where they'd find some
sorta shelter."

He looked at Sha-Wo, who was wearing the blue peak-
crowned cap and jacket that identified him as a member of
the Indian Police. Longarm still had on the flat-crowned
wide-brimmed hat, butternut jeans and blue flannel shirt
he'd put on for traveling after he and the Ponca chieftain
finished their testimony at a trial before the Indian Com-
mission. They had not learned that Sha-Wo's wife had
been abducted until their return to the Ponca settlement,
and Sha-Wo had not removed the ceremonial garment in
their hurry to start after the kidnapped woman.

Now Longarm asked his companion, "Don't you figure
you maybe better skin outa that coat and put it and your

1

cap in your saddlebag? If Ka-No's got your woman in that shanty up ahead, all he needs is a look at that uniform to start him shooting.''

"No!" Sha-Wo exclaimed. "I wear my uniform because it gives me pride! I will not put it aside to go against an outlaw, not even one as bad as Ka-No! Besides, he will shoot at us when he sees us whether I have the coat on or not!''

"Well, I got to admit you're right about him shooting,'' Longarm agreed. "And I sure ain't going to push at you to do something you don't want to, so let's just go on like we are.''

They set their mounts into motion again, and studied the little building as they approached it. The distance was still too great to allow them to make out any of its details, but even in silhouette against the evening sky they could tell that it was crumbling. As they drew swiftly closer they could see that wind and weather had cracked away the upper corners of its walls. The two window openings visible from the spot where Longarm and Sha-Wo approached had neither sash nor glass, and one entire wall of the house was beginning to lean inward.

They'd covered perhaps half the distance to the house when almost at the same time they spotted the sparse clump of green rising from the rolling prairie ahead and reined toward it. As small and low as the brush spot was, it was also the only cover that could be seen in the rolling land that extended to the west like a pointing finger from the broad rectangle of the Indian Nation, now a score of miles behind them.

Both Longarm and Sha-Wo reined toward the spot of green. As they drew closer to it they could see that it was a low clump of spindly and thinly leaved shoots sprouting from the high jagged stump of a live oak tree. They reached the greenery and reined in. Still in the saddle, their heads were above the tallest of the shoots and they dismounted quickly. Then they pulled aside the small sparse live-oak limbs to study the building ahead.

Though the sky was still a clear deep blue in the east and was swiftly losing its sunset glow in the west, the stars had not yet appeared. No matter how he strained to see, Longarm could make out no movement through the slits to which the windows were reduced by angle and distance.

"I know the house," Sha-Wo told Longarm. "It has been here a very long time. The squatters who built it left even before our people were moved here. This country we ride across now, it should have been part of our tribe's allotment instead of being called No-Man's-Land and being forbidden to us, as it is now."

"It don't make no never-mind whose land it oughta be, Sha-Wo," Longarm pointed out. "Even if it is off your reservation you got every right in the world to be here, seeing as how we're chasing an outlaw that ran off with your squaw."

"We must not wait to go after them, Longarm. It will be dark soon, and I would not want Da-Le-Sah to be hurt."

No further words were needed to decide the course of their actions. The Ponca chieftain nodded toward the live-oak stump, them moved his arm in a wide sweeping circle to indicate the northwest before tapping himself on the chest. Longarm's reply was also a nod.

Sha-Wo was eager, and even before Longarm could take a stride to pick up the reins of his companion's horse, the Ponca was crouching and moving at a half-run in a wide

3

circle that would soon bring him to the side of the house, opposite Longarm's position beside the live-oak stump.

Longarm watched him for a moment, then tethered both their mounts to the stub of the tree and began inching carefully in the opposite direction. He moved at an angle that would allow him to see two walls of the hut, and would also force anyone shooting from the ruined adobe's interior to expose himself by having to stand in the window in order to aim a rifle along one of the walls.

Even before Longarm had gotten halfway to the spot for which he was heading, Sha-Wo was lost to sight in the fast-gathering dusk. Somewhere out of sight beyond the crumbling walls of the cabin, Longarm knew that the Ponca chieftain had found cover and was watching, just as he was. He moved faster, almost running now that he'd covered the greater part of the distance to the location he'd selected.

Longarm's burst of speed came just in time. He'd taken only three or four fast steps when the sharp crack of a rifle broke the quiet air and a slug kicked up dust from the prairie beyond him. Longarm was too combat-wise to stop or slow down. He leaped, moving ahead in two giant strides that took him to the position he'd already chosen, a clump of tall prairie grass that was the only hint of cover he'd seen in the barren land.

A second shot broke the sunset silence as Longarm dived behind the grass clump and flattened himself out on the hard ground. This time the slug sailed over him, its threatening hissing whistle telling him to hug the ground in case the sniper inside the ruined adobe made still another try.

Then Sha-Wo's rifle barked from the prairie beyond the adobe, and after silence had hung heavily over the scene

4

for a moment, another shot sounded from the ruined cabin. This time no slug whistled above Longarm, and he knew that the man in the adobe had switched his attention to the threat Sha-Wo now represented.

Silence returned. Longarm waited patiently, but there were no more shots either from Sha-Wo or the man in the ruined adobe. Longarm raised his head and started to rise from the prone position he'd been holding for the past several moments.

Somewhere in the near distance a johnny-owl's rasping cry broke the dying day's stillness. When the bird's first raucously nasal screech reached his ears, Longarm tensed and moved in an instinctive reaction. He raised the muzzle of his Winchester and gathered his legs under him ready to leap up and shoot at the first indication of motion from the cabin.

Even before the owl finished the first full note of its cry, Longarm recognized the silence-breaking noise for what it was and began to worm his way back toward the jagged stump of the lightning-blasted live-oak.

During the few minutes that had ticked past since the first shots were fired the quick prairie twilight had set in. Already the day's last narrowing luminous streaks of pinkish grey were all that brightened the fading daylight sky in the west. The sides of the adobe hut were now in semi-darkness, their position shown only by the glow that seeped grudgingly through the glassless windows.

Longarm moved carefully through the thickening gloom. He divided his attention between the prairie where Sha-Wo's last shot had come from and the blocklike bulk of the adobe hut. He'd covered about a third of the distance, straining his eyes as he tried to force his vision to pierce

5

the failing light, when he glimpsed a darker shadow than usual through one of the windows.

Instinct rather than certainty guided him. Longarm brought up his Winchester and snapped a quick shot at the shadow. His eyes still fixed on the window opening, Longarm's hands moved with the swift ease of familiarity as he pumped a fresh round into the chamber of his Winchester.

With startling suddenness, Longarm realized that the window no longer showed the darker blob of half-seen motion that had prompted his shot. Ignoring the risk, he raised his voice to call to his companion.

"Sha-Wo!" he shouted. "Looks like one of us got him!"

There was no reply from the gloom that had settled now on the area beyond the adobe, no shot from the hut itself. Longarm did not call again, for he knew that Sha-Wo should have replied at once. He started at a half run, half trot, heading for the area beyond the hut where Sha-Wo had taken up his station.

Even before he saw the dark sprawled shape on the dusk-shrouded prairie grass, Longarm knew that he'd been right in guessing what had happened. He walked slowly up to Sha-Wo's body and for a moment stood looking at the dead Ponca. Then he turned away and took the few steps that were needed to reach the adobe.

While the tumbledown front wall had a doorway, there was no door. In spite of the openings for a door and windows, Longarm found the darkness within the one-room house deeper than the gloom outside. He took a match from his vest pocket, and as he raised it above his head so that his hat brim would shield his eyes from the first blinding glare, he rasped the match into flame with his iron-hard thumbnail.

In the sudden quick spurt of light as the match flared up, Longarm saw two horses tethered at one end of the house. The flare dwindled to a steady glow and his eyes adjusted to the light. Now he could see Ka-No's lifeless body lying facedown, spread-eagled on the dirt floor only a step or two distant.

By the time the small flickering flame began to wane he also saw the huddled shapeless heap of a buffalo-hide robe in the farthest corner of the cabin. He let the burned-out match fall and took a long step to the huddled robe before lighting another.

"Da-Le-Sah?" he called. When the buffalo hide moved he bent and grasped a corner of the heavy robe. By now he'd expected to see what was revealed when the hide was pulled aside. Da-Le-Sah, bound and gagged, lay in the corner.

Longarm took out his pocket knife and slashed away the gag and her bonds. She worked her mouth soundlessly for a moment, then said, "Thank you, Longarm. Are you all right?"

"Yes," Longarm answered, "and you don't need to worry anymore about Ka-No. He's laying over there with a bullet in him."

"And Sha-Wo? He is with you, yes?"

Longarm hesitated for a moment.

"Where is Sha-Wo, Longarm, if he is not with you?"

"I hate to tell you this," Longarm replied. The match he held was guttering too close to his fingers for comfort. He let it fall to the dirt floor and burn out while he took another from his pocket and flicked it into life as he had the others. He went on, "Sha-Wo's dead, too. That last shot Ka-No got off killed him."

Da-Le-Sah's expression did not change as she heard

7

Longarm's news. When she said nothing, Longarm said, "Now, listen to me, Da-Le-Sah. There's something that's got to be done, and I'm looking to you for some help."

"What do you wish me to do?"

"Well, most of what's got to be done can wait for morning," Longarm went on. "The job we got to take care of now ain't the nicest thing in the world. It's getting Sha-Wo's body inside here, where the coyotes and wolves can't get to it." Longarm stopped, waiting for Da-Le-Sah to reply. When the match he was holding grew too short he flicked it out and waited in the dark. After he'd almost given up waiting for her to answer, he went on, "I'd sure thank you if you'd give me a hand."

There was another long moment of silence, then Da-Le-Sah replied, "Yes. I will help. It is woman's work to care for the dead. A man should not have to do such things."

Da-Le-Sah moved then, a dark shadow against the brown wall of the adobe hut. Longarm's night vision was returning by the time she started toward him. When she was only a step away he turned and led the way to Sha-Wo's body.

They moved slowly and silently through the darkness. By the time they reached the sprawled figure on the barren ground, their eyes had adjusted and the bright starshine from the cloudless sky provided enough light for them to see well enough to lift the corpse and carry it into the ruined adobe. They placed it beside the wall near the horses and still without speaking moved Ka-No's body beside Sha-Wo's.

"You go ahead and turn in," Longarm said. "Come daylight, we got a pretty good stretch of riding to do."

Looking up at him, her face a blur in the darkness,

Da-Le-Sah asked, "You will go with me back to the Ponca reservation?"

"Well, now, you sure didn't figure on me leaving you to take them bodies back all by yourself. Besides, I'll have to go report to the agency, so they'll know what happened."

"I did not want to ask," Da-Le-Sah said. "But I am glad. Sha-Wo's other wives will be glad too, when they see that his friend did not leave me to bring him home by myself."

"You know, it sorta slipped my mind that Sha-Wo had more'n one wife," Longarm told her. "Once you get back there, you ain't going to be lonesome. Now, you go ahead and turn in. I got two horses out on the prairie that I got to lead back here and put with the others, where the coyotes and bobcats won't spook 'em in the dark."

Though there was no moon, the stars were bright in the clear night air. Longarm had little trouble in spotting the stub of the live-oak and the small sprawl of fresh growth that was rising around its roots. He led the horses back to the tumbledown adobe, and even before he reached it he could hear the low monotonous hum of Da-Le-Sah's voice raised in the death chant.

When he got to the hut, Longarm realized that at some time after he'd left, Da-Le-Sah had led the other two horses outside and tethered them to the skeleton of a door frame before she'd begun her chant. He tethered the pair he was leading beside them without removing their saddles, then stood in the doorway for a moment watching Da-Le-Sah. She was sitting with crossed legs beside Sha-Wo's blanket-covered body, chanting in her low rhythm, her voice pitched only a bit above a whisper as she swayed back and forth.

She paid no attention to Longarm. He stepped back

outside and took his bedroll off his horse. Spreading the blankets just inside the doorway, Longarm took off his gun belt and stretched out on the blankets. He went to sleep with the faint humming sound of Da-Le-Sah's chant filling his ears.

Midsummer nights were short on the prairie. When Longarm woke, the faint greyish tinge of the false dawn was showing through the glassless windows of the ruined adobe hut, and the low rhythmic chant of Da-Le-Sah's death chant still sounded.

Longarm glanced at Da-Le-Sah, saw that she had not changed position, and stepped outside. He walked a short distance away from the hut to stretch his legs. The true dawn was pushing its way above the flat eastern horizon, merging its brightness with the faint shade of grey that had filled the sky earlier.

Taking out one of his long slim cigars, Longarm flicked a match into flame before untying the horses and leading them to the one small area where they could graze. He walked idly around until the sun's rim broke the eastern horizon. A few minutes after the rising sun's yellow light drove off the pre-sunrise grey, the chant from the hut stopped abruptly and Da-Le-Sah appeared in the doorway.

"Good morning, Longarm!" she called to him.

"Morning, Da-Le-Sah."

"I hope you slept well in spite of my chant last night," she went on. "It was my duty to mourn for Sha-Wo."

"Oh, I figured that out, you being his wife and all. And it didn't keep me awake. Anyways, we couldn't've done anything except stay here till daylight. But I'm ready to start back soon as you've rested and feel like riding."

"We must leave very soon," Da-Le-Sah told him.

"Sha-Wo must be buried before sunset, and his other wives must have time to mourn for him."

"Ain't you going to need to rest a little before we set out?" Longarm frowned. "You ain't had a bit of sleep."

"I will be all right," she assured him. "And when we get to our village, Sha-Wo's older wives will take care of the other things that must be done. I can rest then."

"If that's what you're set on doing, I ain't going to try and stop you," Longarm told her. "You just sorta take it easy and I'll get the horses loaded up right away. Then soon as I finish loading, we'll head on back to the Nation."

Longarm took a last puff from his smoked-down cigar, dropped the butt and ground out the last vestige of its glowing coal with the sole of his boot. Around him the small houses and the few remaining tepees of the elderly Poncas who clung to the tribe's olden ways were dark and silent.

"Old son," he said into the darkness, "It's time for you to go inside and hit the hay. Billy Vail won't make too much of a fuss about you having stayed here in the Indian Nation long enough to see Sha-Wo buried proper, but you need to cut a shuck back to Denver tomorrow or Billy's liable to boil over."

Feeling his way through the greater darkness of the little cabin where the dead man's elder wives and Da-Le-Sah had insisted he stay, Longarm located the foot of the iron bedstead and stood beside it while he levered out of his boots and stripped to his long johns.

Out of habit, he carried his gun belt with him as he edged along the bedside to the chair where he'd placed his wake-up cigar, and hung the gun belt across its back where the butt of his holstered Colt would be within easy reach.

11

He laid back and started to stretch luxuriously at the comfort of a mattress under him instead of the hard ground or harder floorboards. His stretch was never completed. A hand closed over his mouth, and in instant reaction he rolled away, his hand reaching for the Colt.

"Longarm! Please! It's only me!"

When Longarm recognized Da-Le-Sah's voice, he let his muscles relax and fell back on the mattress. He relaxed more slowly than he'd tensed at the unexpected touch, but now he no longer struggled.

"I did not want to startle you," Da-Le-Sah went on as she removed her hand from his mouth. Her voice was pitched low, just above a whisper. "But I did not want you to shout and disturb the village, either."

"I got to admit you spooked me for a minute, Da-Le-Sah," Longarm said. "I wasn't expecting to find nobody in bed here, most especially you. Ain't it a little bit soon after Sha-Wo just being buried for you to come calling?"

"Perhaps," she replied. "But not too soon for me. I did not bed with Sha-Wo for three months before Ka-No took me away. I was his number-three wife, not as much a wife to Sha-Wo as a servant to Mi-Ke-Tah and Pah-Se. And Ka-No did not touch me in the few hours I was forced to be with him."

While Da-Le-Sah was talking her hand had been moving down Longarm's muscular torso to his crotch. The soft stroking of her busy fingers was beginning to bring a response, and the matter-of-fact explanation of her position in her dead husband's family changed Longarm's first reaction to her unexpected visit.

"I didn't think a lot about the things you've been telling me," he said. As he spoke, Longarm shifted his position, stretching out comfortably on his back. His groin was

12

stirring now as Da-Le-Sah continued her caresses. "But I guess that does make a lot of difference."

"Then you will let me stay?" she asked.

"I ain't one to turn a lady out, even when she's come to call on me without being invited." Longarm was stripping off his long johns as he talked. "Suppose you just stretch out alongside of me here and we'll get a lot better acquainted."

Da-Le-Sah abandoned her caresses for the moment needed to pull her shift over her head and stretch out beside him. Then her hand returned to the gentle pulsed stroking that had been momentarily interrupted. Now, with her warm hands caressing his bare flesh, Longarm responded very quickly.

A deep sigh burst from Da-Le-Sah's throat when Longarm bent over to find the budded tips of her high firm breasts with his lips. As he applied his kisses he began to caress her breasts' firm undersides with his fingertips and her hips began writhing. Urgently, she pressed her warm body against him. Longarm lifted himself and she slid beneath him, her hand placing his swollen shaft. He plunged and she cried out softly as he drove into her.

Longarm stroked slowly at first, long deliberate thrusts that brought full response from Da-Le-Sah. He did not increase the tempo of his drives until her body began trembling, then he thrust a bit faster, still penetrating with the full length of his swollen shaft. When Da-Le-Sah began writhing and moaning, he speeded up.

Now her soft half-smothered mouthings grew more and more urgent. Longarm began driving with all the vigor of his muscular frame until at last Da-Le-Sah's body tensed them jerked spasmodically, and her cries became a column of sound rising from her throbbing throat. Her hips heaved, her body writhed, and Longarm drove with all his strength in the few finishing strokes that brought them both to a shuddering final spasm which rippled through their joined bodies and drained them to the utmost.

They lay quietly for a while without separating. At last Da-Le-Sah whispered, "Again, soon, Longarm?"

"Sure," he agreed. "Right now, if you've a mind to."

"Now is good," she said. "And later will be even better."

Then Longarm stopped her with his lips as he began the long deliberate strokes she'd invited, starting them up the slope to the ultimate peak of final ecstasy.

Chapter 2

When Longarm entered the outer room of the U.S. marshal's Denver Headquarters he had an immediate hunch that something was brewing. The door to Chief Marshal Billy Vail's private office had been left ajar and Vail was sitting at his desk. Before Longarm had a chance to say good morning to the pink-cheeked young clerk at the desk beside the hall door, Vail's voice sounded.

"Come on in here right his minute, Long!" he called. "And I hope you've brought your report on whatever kind of fracas you got into down in the Indian territory. That rag of Bonfils and Tammens had a story on the front page this morning about some wild shooting match you had with a Ponca outlaw down in the Nation, and I hadn't heard a word about it from you!"

"I wasn't doing anything but helping one of my old friends who belonged to the Indian Police, Billy!" Longarm protested as he started across the room to Vail's office. "He asked me to lend him a hand, or I'd've stayed clear of it. And I didn't talk to no *Denver Post* reporter down there, either!"

"Damn it! You know how touchy the Indian Bureau is in Washington about us getting mixed up with the Indian Police!" Vail went on as Longarm pulled his favorite chair up to the desk and settled into it. "Now I'll be getting messages on the telegraph wire' for a week or more, until things cool off!"

"Well, if you'll just listen to the way things happened, I imagine what I done down in the Nation won't look so bad, even to them idiots back East," Longarm said. "Now, here's how it all came about."

For the next ten or fifteen minutes, Vail listened while Longarm sketched the sequence of events that had gotten him into the shoot-out with the Ponca outlaw. As the story drew to a close the chief marshal nodded and sighed with relief.

"I'd say everything you did made sense," he agreed. "It's just about what I'd've done myself. But watch your step pretty close on this next case you'll be going out on, because it's a real ticklish business."

"You ain't sending me out again on a case the Indians are mixed up with, are you, Billy?" Longarm asked.

"You won't find any redskins where you're going," Vail assured him. "But it's likely to be ticklish, because a bunch of higher-ups in the Treasury Department and the State Department are in it up to their ears, and on top of that I've got a hunch the White House has some strings tied into it."

"You mean I'm going out again right away, Billy? I was figuring I'd have time when I got back here to send out my wash and have some clean clothes to take along when I went on my next job. I ain't got a clean shirt to my name and all my long johns are gummed up with sweat, and my—"

"Your washwoman will need two days to wash and dry and iron your clothes," Vail broke in.

"That's right, Billy. How'd you know I was going to say that?"

"Because I remember what you've told me before," Vail said. "Now I'll tell you what I want you to do. Go buy yourself some new shirts and long johns. Put whatever money you spend on an expense voucher, and I'll approve it when you turn it in."

Longarm was silent for a moment, then he shook his head, and when he spoke his voice was serious. "You sure wouldn't tell me to do that on anything but a big case. Am I right or wrong?"

"You're right this time, Long. There's a lot of money involved in it, and money means important people."

"I guess you better tell me about it, then."

"Close the door before I start. You never know who's going to walk in the outer office while we're talking."

As Vail reached into his desk drawer and produced an oversized manila envelope dotted with blobs of red sealing wax, Longarm closed the door and settled back, lighting a fresh cheroot. Vail upended the envelope on his desk and began to separate the stack of papers that spewed out of it. He found the one he was looking for and passed it over to Longarm.

"Have you ever run into one of these before?" he asked.

"Not as I can recall." Longarm frowned. "But I know what it is, because I heard about 'em when the war was going on. It's a Confederate States government bond, one they put out so they could buy what they needed for the war."

"That's right," Vail agreed. "I've seen damn few myself."

"Why, I never even knew anybody back then that had

17

what this bond cost!'' Longarm exclaimed. ''A hundred thousand dollars is more cash than I'll likely ever see in one pile.''

''It didn't cost that much during the war,'' Vail said. ''Maybe half of that, which is still a lot of money.''

''But it says a hundred thousand right here!''

''That's what the Confederate government promised to redeem it for if the South had won.''

Longarm scanned the green print on the heavy parchmentlike paper and said thoughtfully, ''I reckon a hundred thousand dollars is still a lot of money, Billy.''

''Of course it is! But a war costs a lot,'' Vail went on. ''And there were a lot of real rich planters and bankers in the South back before the war. They figured the South would win, of course. Then they'd get back twice as much as they'd paid.''

''Likely it wasn't just the rich folks that bought these,'' Longarm opined. ''I guess a lot of little storekeepers and farmers squeezed and strained to buy 'em, hoping to get double their money back.''

''Sure they did,'' Vail agreed. ''But now unfold that bond and look at the back of it.''

Longarm opened the crisply crackling folds of heavy paper and studied it for a moment. Then with a frown growing on his face he said, ''I don't get this at all, Billy. Am I right in what I make out this means, that this Barclay's Bank in London put out this bond?''

''That's the size of it,'' Vail said. ''If your memory's as good as mine, you'll know that England was pretty much on the South's side.'' He selected a folded sheaf of paper from the mass of papers that he'd scattered on the desktop and extended it to Longarm as he went on, ''Now, look at this one.''

Longarm glanced at the bond and frowned. "It looks just like the other one to me," he said. "One time it was worth the hundred thousand dollars in gold that the Confederate States said they'd pay to get it back. But there ain't no Confederate States any longer, Billy. This ain't worth nothing but the paper it's printed on."

"Take a closer look," Vail suggested. "Unfold it and look at the back."

Longarm unfolded the stiff paper and scanned the fine print. He looked up and told Vail, "It's just like the other one, Billy."

"Not exactly," Vail said. "Read it again, then look at the back page of the first one I gave you."

After he'd unfolded the bond and glanced quickly at the fine print on its reverse side Longarm began, "I sure don't see—" He stopped short and reread a line or two, then went on, "I guess I missed something when I looked at it the first time. On this one, it says that Barclay's Bank in London, England, will pay a hundred thousand dollars for it."

"And that's the big difference," Vail explained. "There's not any such thing as the Confederate States today, but Barclay's Bank is still doing business in London, and what they did when they issued that bond was to guarantee that the bank would redeem it any time it was brought in."

"Even twenty years or so after the South lost the war?"

"Twenty years or a hundred years, it wouldn't make any difference. There's no time limit set," Vail replied. "If you took that bond in tomorrow to Barclay's and asked them for the hundred thousand dollars it promises, they'd be legally bound to give you the money."

"Then they'd be out a whole heap of cash if there's many of this kind of bond still around."

"That's what's got the Treasury people all upset," Vail went on. "From what our chief says in the letter I got along with all this other stuff, there've been five or six of those bonds brought in the Barclay's Bank in Galveston, Texas lately."

"And the bank had to pony up with all that money?"

"Not yet," Vail said, a mirthless smile crinkling his face. "You see Barclay's Bank in London says that they have no branches in Galveston. They asked the Treasury Department to look into it. Treasury sent a Secret Service Agent down to look into things, but he disappeared. Now they want you to find out what happened to him."

"They ain't asking for much, are they?"

"I imagine they'd settle for less, but what I've just told you is what you're supposed to do."

"How come the U.S. Marshal's office down in Houston ain't doing anything about investigating?"

"You know the Secret Service," Vail replied sourly. "They don't even let their own men know what's going on, so they sure as hell wouldn't be telling us. But my guess is that they want men on this job that the local crooks won't recognize right off."

"Well, the least thing they could do is tell us about it, if that's the situation," Longarm said. "There's times when I think us and the Secret Service ain't even on the same side, Billy."

"So do I. And so do a lot of the rest of us around the country. Speaking of that, you be sure to drop in at Pete Clanahan's office when you get there. Give him my regards, and let him know you're there. But send your reports to me."

"I'll sure do that, Billy. But tell me this: How'd Barclay's of London end up with an old branch in Galveston in the first place?''

"It's not too big a surprise," Vail answered. "Galveston was one of the biggest ports the South had during the war. There were a lot of English ships putting in there with supplies for the Confederate Army.''

"I only been to Galveston a time or two," Longarm said, a sour expression on his face. "Hot and muggy all the time, you feel like you just got out of a bathtub and ain't dried off yet.''

"And I've been there myself," Vail shot back. "But the damned ugly weather goes with the job.''

"Sure." Longarm nodded. "I guess you figure I oughta be leaving right away?''

"I want you to be on the night train south," Vail agreed. "Take both of those bonds with you, just in case you need to be sure that any you run into matches the good one.''

"I ain't sure that's a good idea, Billy," Longarm argued. "What if I lose this good one, or something happens to it? I'd be sure to get the blame for it, and them high muckety-mucks back in Washington would be hounding me to pay for it.''

"That'll just make you be careful not to let it get away from you," Vail replied tartly. Then he grinned and went on, "I've got orders in writing to cover you in case anything might happen to it. Don't worry about it.''

"If you say so, Billy, that's good enough for me.''

Vail nodded and went on, "Henry's fixing up your travel papers and there'll be some extra expense vouchers in with them, because you might have to wind up—well, I'm not going to put any strings on you. The Treasury's paying the bills direct, whatever you're out won't be charged against my office expense.''

"Why, that's real thoughtful of you, Billy," Longarm told his chief. "It almost makes me feel better about having to turn right around and head south again." He stood up. "I guess I better go and start tending to my chores if I'm going to catch that train this evening."

For a man who'd had a broken night's sleep, Longarm felt remarkably chipper when he swung down to the platform of the I&GN depot in Austin and breathed fresh air untainted by the acridity of the coal smoke that had flooded the passenger coach. The trip from Denver had not been a happy one.

Longarm had spent a good part of the first night dozing on a hard bench in the depot at Trinidad, where he'd missed his connection when the tender of the Denver & Rio Grande narrow gauge from Denver had straddled a switch and been stuck for two hours. Finally reaching Abilene, he'd twiddled his thumbs for three hours waiting for a late freight train to clear the single track to Austin on the I&GN. Now he was hungry and sleepy and his temper was short, but the thought that he was at least halfway to his destination was beginning to brighten his mood, just as the breaking dawn was brightening into day.

Glancing up the tracks toward the baggage car, Longarm saw his rifle and saddlebags being handed to the conductor by the man in the baggage car, and made a beeline along the coaches to claim his property. Then, as he'd learned to do early in the course of his extensive railroad travels, he hurried back to the depot door and looked at the train schedule chalked on the blackboard beside it.

A frown spread over Longarm's face as he read the

22

scrawled message it held. The words did nothing to raise his spirits. In the column devoted to passenger trains, the stationmaster had lettered, "Southbound I&GN #32 — 4 hrs late, derailment."

"Now, ain't that a pretty how-dee-do!" Longarm told himself under his breath. "Two damn trains off the track first shot outa the barrel! That board says four hours late, but it more'n likely means six, maybe longer. And what in hell is a man going to do at this time of day in a place like Austin?"

Even as he was muttering, the solution popped into his mind. He picked up his rifle and saddlebags and carried them to the street side of the depot. As he'd expected, two or three livery carriages stood at the hitch rail in front of the station, the cabbies dozing in the front seats of their rigs. Picking out the cleanest looking of the three, Longarm stepped over to it and shook the sleeping driver.

"Wake up, friend," he said. "I want a ride to the headquarters of the Texas Rangers, wherever it is right now."

"It was still behind the new capitol yesterday. That's the last time I looked at it, and I don't figure nobody moved it last night," the hackman said. "Cost you four bits unless you're a lawman. If you are, you get half-price fare."

Taking out the folded wallet in which he carried his badge, Longarm flipped it open. The cabbie nodded. "When I set eyes on you I sorta figured you'd be carrying some kinda badge," he said. "You got the looks, all right. Jump in, Marshal. I'll have you at the Ranger station in a jiffy."

Though Longarm tried to relax and be comfortable as the livery rig bounced over the uneven brick paving on Congress Avenue, the jolting of the hack's thinly padded

23

seat kept him from enjoying the ride. He heaved a sigh of relief as the liveryman reined his horse onto the unpaved but smooth dirt road that circled the still-unfinished capitol. The driver reined away from the big rectangle of massive granite blocks after circling half of it, and a few moments later pulled up in front of a square squat structure of hewn limestone. Lights spilled from half the windows, the others were dark.

"Here you are, Marshal," the hackie announced. "And I guess there's some kind of excitement going on, or the place wouldn't be lighted up so early."

"I'll know soon enough, I suppose," Longarm said, paying the hackman before pulling his saddlebags and rifle out of the cab. "I don't aim to be here long. Just visiting an old friend of mine between trains."

"Well, if you want me to pick you up and take you back to the depot—" the cabman began.

"I'll find my way back all right, but thanks just the same."

As the hackie nodded and turned his horse to leave, Longarm lifted his saddlebags and went into the building. The short hall that he entered had doors on each side. He headed for the door where a light showed through the transom and went in without knocking. At the rear of the sparsely furnished room, a man stood in front of a rack of rifles, reaching for one of the weapons. Though he was standing with his back to the door, Longarm recognized him at once.

"Looks like you're getting ready to go someplace, Will," he said.

Without turning his head the man at the gun rack swiveled around, his hand darting to the butt of his holstered Colt. When he saw Longarm he grinned a bit sheepishly.

24

As he dropped his hand he said, "Well, I'll be damned! Longarm! It's been such a long time since I've seen you that I knew your voice but just couldn't place it."

"You mean you didn't hear me come in the door?"

"Not until you started talking."

"You better put a bell or something on it. You'd be dead meat right now if I'd've been some outlaw out to get even with you," Longarm told him.

"Not much chance of that happening," the Ranger said. He was walking toward Longarm as he spoke. As the two men shook hands, he went on, "No outlaw in his right mind's going to come in here unless one of us drags him in. But how the devil did you know I'd be here?"

"I didn't," Longarm replied. "I had to change trains here and got caught in a layover because the one I'm taking's running late. So instead of cooling my heels at the depot, I figured I'd come out here."

"It'll have to be a short visit, Longarm. I was just getting ready to ride out. But I fixed up a plate of bacon to go with some leftover biscuits to eat, and if you ain't had breakfast you're welcome to sit down for a bite before I leave."

Longarm followed the Ranger to a desk where the plate of bacon and biscuits waited. They sat down and munched in silence for a moment, then Longarm asked, "What kind of case you going out on, Will?"

"I'm not sure it's really a case yet. I got a tip an hour or so ago about a gang we've been after for the last three months, but I won't know how good it is till I go out and run it down. Before I can leave I've got to rouse up Sam Davis and tell him to look after the office here while I'm away."

"Sounds like you're sorta running things around here now," Longarm commented.

"You might say so," the Ranger said. "I got promoted since I saw you the last time, Longarm. I'm Sergeant Will Travers now."

"Well, congratulations! You'll make a good officer for the captain."

"Thanks. But there's times when I'd just as soon not've been promoted. Like right now. Captain McNelly's out on a case up in the Panhandle, so I'm in charge until he gets back. I'm supposed to stay close to the office, but the thing is, I've only got two men here right now, and both of 'em are crippled up so bad they can't ride."

"But not bad enough to keep 'em from looking after things while you go out on this new case?"

"Sam Davis has got a busted leg and has to hobble around on a crutch. Charlie Casey's still in bed. He's getting over a bullet that went through his belly in a gunfight with a bunch of rustlers that's been plaguing the ranchers over to the east side of the county. Neither one of 'em could do anything much if I got into any kind of jackpot."

"How many rustlers you figure on running into?"

"There's at least six. Maybe more. I don't know for sure."

"How much of a ride is it to where you'll be going?" Longarm asked, frowning.

"It's not far. The gang's supposed to be sheltering in some caves about a good hour's ride from town."

"An hour out and an hour back," Longarm said thoughtfully. "Tell you what, Will. I got four hours to wait for my train, and likely a little bit longer than that. If you got

26

a horse and saddle gear to fix me up with, I'll go along and back you up."

"Are you sure you can spare the time?" Travers asked.

"Well, if I miss the train it won't put me out a bit to wait for the next one. I'm not due to get to where my case is on any sort of schedule."

"It'd be good to ride with you on a case again, Longarm."

"By that, I take it you can fix me up with a nag and a saddle?"

"Sure as shooting, I can! The stable's right out in back. I'll go tell the boys they're to look after the office, and we'll be on our way soon as we can saddle up!"

Chapter 3

"Maybe you better tell me a little bit more about this gang we're going after," Longarm suggested as he and Will Travers rode through the cool morning air.

As yet the sun had not risen high enough to be out of their faces and the two men were heading directly into its bright yellowish rays. They kept their heads tilted downward to protect their eyes in the half-circle of shade cast by their hat brims.

"It's a new bunch of outlaws that's got together during the past four or five months," Travers said. "So far we don't know who the leader is, or even if they've got one. But they've been getting away with more steers than you'd imagine from the ranches east of here, and I've got a hunch that they were mixed up in a bank holdup over at Bastrop about three months ago."

"You said there were maybe five or six of 'em?"

"As far as we can figure out," the Ranger said. "And I've sorta suspicioned they might be using the bee caves to hide out in between jobs or maybe as a place to get together before they go out on one."

"Bee caves?" Longarm asked. "If that means what I take it to, you tell me which caves has got bees in 'em. I aim to stay clear of them buzzing pests. I got enough bee

29

stings when I was a little tad back in West Virginia to last me as long as I live.''

"Oh, hell, Longarm! That's just what the folks around here call 'em. I guess there used to be a few bees' nests in some of the caves way back when, maybe during the Indian days, but that was before my time.''

"And you're sure the bees have all gone by now?''

"As sure as I can be.''

"That's all right, then," Longarm said nodding. For the next few moments the two men rode ahead in silence, then he turned to the Ranger and asked, "I guess it's occurred to you that some of them outlaws might be hands on the ranches hereabouts?''

"That was the first thing Captain McNelly said, too. He's got an idea that this bunch might be working some new kind of scheme.''

"I thought I'd run onto all the dodges outlaws use to hide," Longarm said. "But maybe McNelly's tumbled onto one I ain't come across. You feel like telling me what it is?''

"I don't suppose the captain would mind," Travers answered. "His idea is that between their jobs the whole bunch just drifts along a ways, then they scatter out and get jobs at spreads that ain't too far apart for 'em to get together easy. They pull a job here and another one there and the next one someplace else, then they scatter out again and start all over wherever they light next.''

"Now, that hadn't occurred to me," Longarm said with a thoughtful frown. "But it might be. I done a lot of drifting when I was a mite younger than I am now, and I was always running into some hand I'd got acquainted with when I was on a different job. Drifting's got to be a sorta habit for a lot of wranglers anymore.''

"Trains make it easier than it used to be. But the captain's idea makes sense," Travers went on. "A stray hand stops at one of the spreads and has a meal—there's not a spread anyplace I know about that'll turn away a stranger—and he'll likely say he's looking for a job, but all the time he's sizing up the herd and the lay of the land."

"It's sure easier for a hand to move around anymore," Longarm agreed. "I run into a lot of drifters, just like I guess you Rangers do. And the trouble is, a rancher don't know it, but that drifter might be getting the lay of the land, seeing how many hands are working a spread, and then the first thing that the rancher knows, he's lost maybe fifteen or twenty head outa one of his range herds."

While Longarm and Travers were talking the land had taken on a pronounced upward slant. The nature of the country itself had changed. When they'd first set out, they'd ridden across land covered by thin curls of short growth and dotted with small stands of tall cottonwood trees. Occasionally where the brush thinned there'd been the tall nodding stalks of bluebonnets.

Now the grama grass was growing thinner, and mesquite clusters were appearing. Some of the feathery leaved trees were little more than saplings; a few grew from trunks as big as a man's arm, others spurted up finger-thin and spindly. Bluebonnets grew among the trees in patches, some only a few feet from end to end or side to side, others filling an area that could not be covered by a bedsheet.

Here and there the bare ground was exposed. The soil had changed its hue now; it was a light yellow and broken by low ragged stretches of grey-white rock on which nothing could take root. Spreading away from the crumbly sandstone, irregular clusters of olive-green cow's-tongue cactus twinkled with small yellow flowers and the glistening of long brownish needles.

"How much farther we got to go to get to them caves you were talking about?" Longarm asked.

"Not much farther," Travers replied. He pointed ahead, where the ground rose abruptly to what appeared to be a sharp ragged crest. "Once we get past that ridge we hit a big patch of limestone that's split up into five or six little canyons. The caves are in that stretch. Mostly you'll find 'em opening up in the canyons. We won't bother with the little ones, just those that're big enough to drive steers through."

"So far, I ain't seen any sign that anybody's ridden over this stretch of ground since the year one," Longarm commented.

"Yep, you run into that a lot around here," the Ranger explained. "Either it's too hard to take prints or too soft to hold 'em. That's why we're making a beeline to the caves. Anyplace else, we'd have some hoofprints to guide us, but this ain't like most places."

"I'll put in with you on that," Longarm agreed. "Makes a fellow wonder where he's at, sometimes."

"It takes some getting used to," Travers agreed. "But I've been here long enough to sorta know my way around. This is one of the places hereabouts where a man that's wanted real bad will make a beeline for. The trouble we've got is that the outlaws know how the land lays better than most of us Rangers do."

"That's most always how it is." Longarm nodded. "And it ain't that they're that much smarter. It's just because there's always a lot more of them than there is of us."

They'd reached the top of the rise now, and reined in. Longarm could see at a glance that Travers had not exaggerated his description of the terrain ahead. Sliding one of his long thin cigars out of his pocket, Longarm flicked his thumbnail over a match head and lighted up. There was no wind, and the smoke from the cigar rose straight up as he examined the rock outcrop.

Crest after low crest of jagged white limestone ridges stretched as far as he could see. There was very little difference in their height, though here and there a crest rose to a peak like a truncated steeple that jutted above those on either side of it. Except for the difference in color and the lack of motion, Longarm might have thought he was on a seashore looking out across a wind-tossed ocean that was midway between rough and calm.

"It's sure one hell of a place to ride over," he commented. "You figure these nags are up to it?"

"No. Not for very long, anyhow. What we'd better do is cover this stretch on foot. You stay here and I'll ride up ahead a ways before I stop. The thing to look for is horse droppings. They show up so good against all that light-colored rock that you can spot 'em real easy."

"How far across do you want to go?"

"Hell, this whole stretch ain't more'n a quarter mile wide," Travers replied. "We oughta be able to cover it in, oh, say an hour or so."

"I'll sorta keep track of the time, then, and you do the same thing, and I'll look for you to come back in an hour, give or take a few minutes."

"Good. Let's hope one of us finds what we're looking for."

Travers reined ahead and Longarm dismounted. He found

33

a big stone that he used to weigh down his horses's tether and was slipping his rifle out of its saddle scabbard when it occurred to him that in the cramped foreshortened quarters of a cave the Winchester might well be a handicap. He pushed the gun back into its scabbard and stepped out across the first limestone ridge.

Surprisingly, the stone underfoot was as abrasive as sandpaper, and Longarm had no trouble making his way across the first ridge that he crossed. He walked up it in one direction, then retraced his steps, looking for the dark opening that would mark a cave, but saw none. Nor did he see any vestiges of manure that would mark the passing of a horse and rider.

Walking along the bottom of the vee-shaped gulley he looked at the similar gullies on both sides, keeping his eyes peeled for the telltale signs of either caves or horses. When he could see the end of the rock formation ahead, Longarm turned and crossed to the next gully and began retracing his steps, marking his progress by glancing now and then at his tethered horse.

It was not until he'd crossed the second ridge that he saw in the white rock a black blob that marked a cave. The opening was large enough to allow a man to pass through, but too small to accomodate a horse. He stepped across the spine of the adjacent ridge and made his way to the dark mouth.

A quick look revealed no signs that anyone had been in the vicinity lately, but Longarm decided he would take no chance of missing a vital spot. He crossed to the mouth of the cavern and bent over it, his eyes searching the areas of whitish-grey stone around it. Only a few minutes of observation was required. The surface of the rock around the cave showed neither the freshly scraped marks that horseshoes would make nor the less prominent scratches that would have been left by a man's boot heels.

His observation of the area did reveal another cave opening fifty or sixty yards distant. It was larger than the one he'd just finished investigating, and he started toward it. He'd taken only a step or two when the sharp, high-pitched crack of a rifle broke the quiet morning air, and the deeper, more resonant roar of a pistol followed.

Longarm was already halfway to the crest of the ridge. He took the two long steps needed to bring him up to its spine and looked in the direction that Will Travers had taken. A flicker of movement caught his eyes. He concentrated on the spot where it had appeared and was waiting patiently when the rifle cracked again. Longarm started in the direction from which the shot had sounded, but he'd taken only a few steps when Travers's head and shoulders appeared above the rim of the ridge ahead.

Longarm had drawn his Colt at the sound of the shot. He put it back into its holster now and called, "I guess you got off the last shot just then or I wouldn't be looking at you now."

"You're right," the Ranger called back. "It was a tight squeeze, though. If that rustler in the cave had been just a little bit quicker on the draw, you'd be looking at him now instead of me."

"You knew who he was?"

"Not till I looked at him after I'd dropped him. He was one of the rustlers we're after, though. Red Smathers was his name. I left him laying in the cave because I figured you'd hear the shooting and be heading this way."

"You reckon there's more'n one of 'em hiding out along this ridge, Will?"

"Where there's one, there's likely to be more," Travers

replied. "Let's keep looking along here. We just might flush out one or two more of 'em."

"You keep going ahead and I'll double back," Longarm suggested. "If we move apart instead of me following you, we'll be less apt to plug each other."

"That's fine with me," Travers agreed. "There's only two more caves ahead that's big enough for 'em to shelter in, and if I recall rightly there's about three big ones in the direction you'll be going."

"Then we better get at it," Longarm told him. "We'll meet where we left the horses."

Travers acknowledged Longarm's suggestion with a wave and a nod before turning away and starting along the ridge. Longarm began picking his way in the opposite direction over the streak of white stone that rose above the lowland that surrounded it.

He'd covered only a few hundred yards, taking long but careful steps over the hard treacherous rock formation when he saw the black opening of another cavern.

At first glance it looked too narrow for a man to enter, but as he drew closer and could make out details he saw that he'd been mistaken. The slit that had seemed so narrow when he'd glimpsed it was almost wide enough to lead a horse through. He got to the little cut that opened beyond the cave's mouth and slid down to the wide crack.

There were no marks of footprints on the solid rock, but Longarm had not expected to find any. After he'd stood for a careful moment, studying the blackness that began a few yards beyond the opening, Longarm stepped into the yawning crevice. A half dozen steps inside took him to the point where there was no more light ahead, and his own body was blocking out the daylight that flooded through the opening behind him.

Drawing his Colt, Longarm resumed his advance. He moved slowly, stopped now and then to let his eyes adjust to the deepening gloom. He'd reached the point now where daylight merged with darkness, fifteen or twenty feet past the entrance.

As his eyes grew accustomed to the dimmer light, a frown crinkled Longarm's face. In the distance he could see a few pinpoints of brightness. He could not decide whether they came from the sun or from a lantern or candle. The little glints did not provide enough light for him to make out any details of the slit in the area where he stood, but they did provide him with the knowledge that another opening was ahead, Colt ready, he moved slowly forward.

Longarm had taken only a few careful steps when a buzzing sounded close by and something brushed his face. He stopped and another buzz reached his ears, then in quick succession another and still another until his ears were filled with the faint noise that he could not yet identify. A sudden sharp pain stabbed one ear and he felt another pain on his chin, then his cheek.

Raising his free hand, keeping his Colt leveled, it's muzzle pointed toward the tiny points of light that still showed ahead, Longarm brushed at his ears, his cheeks, his chin, but the stabs were multiplying faster than he could move his hand.

"Them's bees!" he exclaimed in the darkness. "Old son, you've run into a damn beehive!"

By now the air around Longarm was beginning to hum, and fresh darts of pain were prickling at his cheeks and the narrow strip of skin on his forehead between his hat brim and his eyebrows. The pain from the stings was increasing. Longarm holstered his Colt and began beating with both hands at his face.

No matter how swiftly he brushed and swatted at the buzzing invisible swarm, he was unable to drive the bees away. Their buzzing was constant now, high-pitched, and the bees continued to cover his face in spite of his efforts to drive them away. He began slapping his cheeks and neck, and he could feel the juices from the bees he killed trickling down his chin.

Longarm's eyelids were swelling fast, beginning to squeeze shut in spite of his attempts to keep them open. Through the slim and rapidly closing slits of the lids he could see only the tiniest of pinpoints from the gleams of daylight for which he'd been heading. In desperation he pulled off his hat and started to beat his cheeks and chin and neck with its brim, but no matter how he flailed and batted and slapped at his face the bees returned.

Instinctively, Longarm opened his mouth to shout, hoping that Will Travers would hear him. Only a faint gurgling sound came from his throat as some of the bees crawled between his parted lips, and he gagged and tried vainly to spit them out in spite of the darting pains that were now stabbing him from stings on his tongue and the insides of his cheeks.

Now the juices of the bees that he managed to crush between his teeth began trickling down his throat. He gagged and began to cough. His instinctive reaction to the pain cleared both the live and the dead bees from Longarm's mouth, but their stings were already burning like coals of fire on his tongue and the insides of his cheeks.

Longarm's eyelids were swollen closed by this time. Though he could see nothing at all, he heard Will Travers shout, and even through swollen lids he could see the red

38

glow of flames and could also smell the acrid odor of smoke.

"Hang on, Longarm!" Travers said. "This smoke'll drive the damn bees away, and I'll get you outa here soon as I can."

Longarm tried to reply, but his tongue had now swelled to such a size that it crowded his mouth and he was unable to control it. His hands and feet were like lead, his head was starting to sag, and his entire body seemed to be one big heap of red-hot coals. He fought hard to keep his senses working and was only dimly aware of Travers supporting him and half carrying, half dragging him through the underground passage.

During the short time required for them to reach the mouth of the cave, the poison that had been discharged into Longarm's bloodstream by the killer bees continued to do its devastating work. He'd been stung far too many times. He heard Travers speak once or twice, but the Ranger's words made only fleeting impressions on his fast-waning awareness of the world around him.

His last feeling was one of burning heat in every inch of his body. Then the venom of the killer bees overcame him and Longarm was lost in a totally blank blackness.

Longarm's consciousness returned slowly. His first impression was one of burning, a less painful heat than he remembered as having been his final feeling before blacking out, but one that was still strong enough to make him uncomfortable.

With sudden surprise he realized that his eyes were open and that he was in a bed in a room strange to him, staring up at a shadowed ceiling. He tried to move his arms and legs, and was a bit surprised but reassured when his fingers moved and his arms lifted without pain while his bare legs brushed against soft smooth cloth. Now Longarm tried to sit up, and for a moment his muscles refused to respond. For an instant worry swept into Longarm's mind, then his arms and legs responded and he sat up.

Though the drawn window curtains filtering the outside light left the room to dimness, it was bright enough for Longarm to examine his surroundings. He was in what he recognized at first glance as being a well-furnished bedroom.

Though the chamber was not large, its walls were adorned with several framed pictures—their subjects only smudged blurs in the dim light—and heavy drapes hung at the windows' sides. The furniture was a suite of dark-stained oak. In addition to the bed there was a bureau with a high-rising mirror, a washstand, a tall wardrobe, a small square table with an unlighted lamp on it, and several chairs. A Turkish carpet covered the floor.

"Well, old son, it looks like you fell into a beehive and by some hook or crook you woke up in a real nice room," Longarm said into the dimness. "But any room at all'd sure be a big sight better'n that cave you were in. Question is now, where in hell are you, and how long you been here, and there don't seem to be nobody around to give you no answers."

Throwing back the sheet that covered him, Longarm turned to swing his legs off the bed. He was sitting there, studying the dim room, wondering where his clothing was, then frowning as he realized that there was no sign of his Colt, his Winchester, or his saddlebags.

He started to stand up, found his legs too shaky to walk or even to hold him in a standing position, and sank back down on the side of the bed. After sitting quietly for a moment he tried once more to stand up, and this time managed to take a half-step away from the bed. While he was debating whether to take another step or to return to the bed, the rattle of the doorknob made the decision for him. As the door opened and a woman came into the room, he managed to turn and dive for the bed and pull the sheet over his shoulders to drape his nakedness.

"Marshal Long!" the woman who'd entered the room exclaimed. "You're not supposed to get out of bed yet!"

"Well, I don't see—" Longarm began. Realizing that he was in no condition or position to argue with a woman he did not know, he fell silent.

"I'm sorry I spoke so sharply," she said apologetically. "I know you must be wondering where you are, and who I am. My name is Nell Colton, and I'm, well, a sort of unofficial aunt or cousin or something of the sort to the Texas Rangers at the headquarters here in Austin."

Longarm was looking at her while she explained. Nell Colton was a tall woman, statuesque. In spite of her white hair, which she wore in a low bun gathered at the back of her head, her face revealed only that she was well past maturity. Under thick brows, her eyes were light blue. Her nose was thin and a bit too small for her face, and lines ran from it in a smooth curve to the corners of her full red lips. Her chin was firm, though softly rounded, and her neckline was unmarred by lines or wrinkles.

"I'm real pleased to meet you, ma'am," Longarm managed to say. "But I came to all of a sudden, and I figured I better find out where I was, or where I am, and how I got here."

"Your Ranger friend, Will Travers, brought you here," she told him. "Late yesterday afternoon. You were in pretty bad shape at the time, but luckily I've taken care of killer bee stings before, and knew what to do. You'll

41

probably be shaky for a little while, but you're perfectly all right. Just lie back down, and I'll go get you something to eat."

Before Longarm could reply or protest, she turned and went out of the room, leaving him staring at the door she'd closed behind her.

Chapter 4

"You know, you're really a very lucky man, Longarm," Nell Colton observed.

She and Longarm were sitting at a small table in the kitchen of her house. Dishes on the table between them held the remains of their shared supper, and Longarm had just lighted one of his cheroots. While chatting during dinner they'd abandoned formality and had begun addressing one another by their first names.

"Oh, I know that, Nell," Longarm replied. "And I don't mind telling you, I sure felt like a goner when those bee stings started getting to me back in that cave."

"They've earned their reputation as killers, all right," she agreed. "You very well might have died if Will hadn't gotten you out as fast as he did."

"I owe Will for saving me, I guess. That just about makes us even, though. I pulled his bacon out of the fire one time a while back, when we were working on a case down in Houston. But I sure owe you a lot for the way you've taken such good care of me when he brought me to your house here."

"You don't owe me a thing," she protested. "You're an unusually strong, healthy man. That's one reason you've made such a quick recovery."

"I'm sure a sight to look at, though," he said, holding up the backs of his hands. They were covered with bumpy red weals. "I took a look in the mirror while I was getting dressed for supper and I couldn't hardly recognize my own face."

"It'll take a day or two for what's left of the swelling to go down, but you're as healthy now as you've ever been."

"That's real good news, Nell. I need to be on my way to take care of the case I started out on when I left Denver."

"Yes, Will Travers told me that you'd just intended to stop here between trains. He said you were having to go all the way down to the Gulf of Mexico."

"That's where my case is," Longarm said, nodding. "When I got here yesterday morning and saw how late the train was that I was figuring to take the rest of the way, I just got the idea that I might as well use the time by going to the Ranger headquarters and seeing who was around."

"You won't have to hurry tomorrow. That morning train doesn't get here until ten o'clock."

"If there ain't anything I can help you with—firewood to bring in or giving you a hand wiping the supper dishes or something like that—"

"Not a thing," Nell broke in. "It's thoughtful of you to offer, but I have a half-day maid who comes in and takes care of the housework."

"I'll bid you goodnight, then," Longarm said as he stood up. "I ain't still so shaky, but I feel like I could use a mite of shut-eye."

"I don't suppose you'll have any trouble waking up in the morning?" Nell asked. "I'm an early riser, and if you'd like for me to call you, I'll be glad to."

"Why, I generally wake up at the crack of dawn myself, but thanks all the same."

"Then I'll see you at breakfast. Goodnight, Longarm."

"Night, Nell. And thanks again for a good supper."

Back in his bedroom, the first thing Longarm noticed was that during the two or three times when she'd excused herself during their supper, Nell Colton had come in to turn down the covers of his bed and to close the window blinds and light the fat candle that stood in its stand on the bureau. He wasted no time in levering out of his boots and shucking off his shirt and trousers.

Stretching and yawning as he stood in the center of the room, Longarm decided that the night was a bit warm for comfort with the blinds closed. Before skinning out of his underwear he attended to the final bedtime precaution that he'd learned to take very soon after beginning his work as a lawman. Living with the constant threat of retaliation from outlaws whose careers in crime he'd interrupted, Longarm had learned to be prepared.

Whether in his familiar room in Denver or on a case in the field, he'd formed the habit of keeping his revolver handy. He pulled the chair close to the head of the bed, took his Colt out of its holsters, and put the weapon in the chair seat where he could reach out and grab it.

Skinning out of his underwear, he blew out the lamp and stepped to the window to open the blinds. He stood for a moment gazing out at the moonlit fields stretching away from the house, then went back to the bed and slipped between the cool, faintly perfumed sheets. Longarm had never been one to need a lullaby. His head had been cradled on the pillow for only a few minutes when slumber took him. He was sleeping peacefully in the deep silent darkness when the clicking of the doorknob brought him instantly awake.

His hand found his Colt in an instant and he was leveling it at the door when he saw a slim white figure slip inside the room. The bright moonlight that flooded through the open window lighted the room brightly enough to enable him to see Nell Colton quite clearly. There was no need for him to guess her reason for coming to his room. The doorway framed her like an artist's portrait, and like many portraits she stood posed completely naked. Longarm let go the breath he'd been holding and laid the revolver back on the chair.

"I wasn't aiming to throw down on you, Nell," Longarm apologized. "But when we said goodnight a little while ago you said something about me not seeing you till breakfast."

"I'm sorry if I startled you," she said. "But I didn't think you'd be asleep yet."

"I'd just dropped off," Longarm told her. "I ain't one to sleep right sound, though." A smile grew on his face as he went on, "Looks to me like we're even-Steven. You were about as surprised to see my Colt as I was to see you come in."

"I'll admit I didn't expect to be looking into the barrel of your pistol," she replied as she walked slowly toward the bed and stood looking down at him. "You don't mind my informal visit, do you?"

"Not one little bit," Longarm assured her. He was staring at Nell's figure with undisguised admiration, hiding his surprise at its youthfulness. Her full breasts stood high, with dark aureoles around their large tips. Despite her snow-white hair, her pubic bush was a coal-black wisp that contrasted sharply with the flood of silvery tresses that fell in a fanned spread over her bare shoulders.

"I'm pretty sure I know what you're thinking right now." She smiled. "Because you must know the reason I came here. But if I'm right in my guess you're wondering about the color of my hair. It began turning white after an illness I had when I was only sixteen."

"You don't look much more'n sixteen to me right now."

"I thank you for the compliment, Longarm," she said with a smile. "But both of us know I'm a bit older than that. Perhaps I'm not quite as old as you've been thinking I am, though. Now, are we going to keep talking the rest of the night, or do I have to invite myself to join you in bed?"

"Why, I'd never turn down a lady as pretty as you, Nell. It don't seem to me like you really need an invitation, but if you do, don't hold back on my account."

Nell walked slowly and deliberately to the bed and sat down on its edge. Longarm lifted himself on an elbow and put his free arm around her shoulders. He pulled her slowly downward until their lips met. He felt her lips part and thrust his tongue to meet hers. As they held their kiss Nell began to quiver, and her hand crept to his crotch to caress his burgeoning erection.

When their kiss had continued until both were breathless, and Longarm had swollen and grown rigid in response to Nell's soft stroking, she turned her head a bit to break the kiss.

"After Will had to leave and go back to Ranger headquarters I took your clothes off to see if you had any bee stings besides the ones on your face and arms," she said. "I didn't quite believe my eyes, and I still don't, but I

47

didn't have time to spend looking. I'm sure you won't mind if I look closer now."

"Whatever pleasures you pleasures me," Longarm told her.

He lay back and propped himself up on his elbows as Nell bent over him. she was in no hurry. She rubbed her cheeks and lips with the tip of Longarm's throbbing swollen shaft before engulfing it with a soft sigh of pleasure, and soon his entire body began growing tense as she continued her expert attentions.

Longarm returned her caresses as best he could, rubbing his callused fingers over the firm pebbled tips of her full soft breasts, but as time passed his tension mounted to the point where pleasure began to become painful. He put his hands under her arms and lifted her as easily as if she'd been a child. While he held her suspended above him, Nell spread her thighs and grasped his throbbing erection to guide it while he lowered her.

Longarm embraced her and held her soft quivering body firmly to his as he rolled to place himself above her, then he began driving. Nell caught his rhythm quickly. She timed the rise of her hips to meet his lusty thrusts, and soft humming sighs began flowing from her lips as Longarm speeded up the tempo of his deep penetrations.

Within a few minutes Nell's humming sighs grew louder. Longarm kept speeding up the tempo of his drives, and as time ticked away her humming became a throaty cry of pleasure. Longarm continued to pound. When he felt Nell beginning to grow tense he increased still more the speed and force of his deep lunges. Then she began trembling. In a moment she screamed, bucking and writhing as Longarm kept driving with long full strokes.

Suddenly Nell began bucking furiously and her murmur

grew to become one loud cry after another. At last her frenzy ebbed and she went limp, but Longarm did not stop stroking. He slowed his thrusts to a milder tempo, and after a few minutes passed Nell stirred beneath him. For a short while she continued to lie passive, sighing and gasping, but soon she began once more to raise her hips to meet his. While time seemed to stand still, Longarm maintained his steady pace and once more Nell's muscles tightened as again the throaty sighs of pleasure began trickling from her lips.

Longarm was reaching finality himself now, and was ready to meet her next climax when it arrived. As Nell began to buck and writhe and her cries of pleasure again started streaming from her lips, Longarm drove with triphammer speed and strength until he heard Nell begin her climactic scream. Then he let go and bucked in a few final thrusts and lurched forward over Nell's soft quivering body where he lay motionless and spent.

Moments grew to minutes and the minutes passed as time stretched. Finally Nell stirred and said, "You're even a lot more man than I'd expected you to be."

"Well, now, I take that as a compliment, Nell, and I thank you, because I can tell that I ain't the only man you been in bed with."

"Certainly not! But I'm enjoying being here with you so much that I don't want to stop."

"What ever gave you the idea that I did, either? We got the whole rest of the night. And when I find a woman that's as sweet and pretty and full of life as you are, I don't aim to waste much time. You just say the word, and we'll start all over again whenever you feel like it."

Almost three years had gone by since Longarm's last visit

to Houston. He no longer recognized any familiar land-marks as he stood in the vestibule of the day coach, looking at the countryside while the I&GN train poked along at a reduced speed on the winding stretch of track that bordered Buffalo Bayou. Instead, he saw rows of neat, freshly painted new houses where on his last visit there had been only a soggy marshland.

He glanced ahead, and was again surprised at the num-ber of sheds and warehouses and new buildings. Most of these were brick, a sharp contrast to the old waterfront, which had been jerry-built of boards or sheet tin or what-ever material was handiest and cheapest.

"Looks like this ain't a one-horse town no longer," he muttered to himself. "And when a place like this grows too fast it pulls every kind of crook to come where they can make a quick killing. You better watch pretty close while you're here, old son. Chances are you might run into more'n one crook that's got his name on the Wanted list."

One building that had not changed was the red sand-stone I&GN depot, though the huge castlelike structure no longer rose from familiar surroundings. For the first few minutes after he'd gotten off the train and stepped outside the station, Longarm simply stood gazing at the strangely varied stream of pedestrians that crowded the narrow brick-paved street. As far as he could see in both directions the area around the depot was crowded with tumbledown, small one- and two-story office and store buildings jammed together cheek by jowl.

When in doubt where to go in a strange town, Longarm knew to fall back on the expedient that had always helped him to get oriented. He stepped out to the line of hackney cabs waiting for fares along the street and stopped at the first one he came to.

"It's been a while since I was here last," he told the hackman. "And the town's grown some since then. I guess I better hire you to take more where I need to go."

"Just tell me where that is and step into the cab," the man on the high seat invited. "I'll guarantee to get you there."

"Before I say yes or no, maybe you better tell me how much traveling around town's going to cost me."

"Depends on you, friend. If you've got a lot of places to go, maybe you better hire my rig by the day."

"How much would that amount to?"

"Us hackmen get three dollars a day now, instead of two. And you won't find none of us that'll work any cheaper."

"It sounds precious high"—Longarm frowned—"but I guess if it's the going rate I'll have to pay it."

"We got a deal, then. Where to, mister?"

"Well, now," Longarm replied, "I got to look in at the Federal Building, then I'll need to stop at Barclay's Bank, and after that I'll be going over to Galveston Island. I guess that means a ferry boat, so you'll have to take me to the landing."

"There ain't no ferry on this side of the bay till you get way down to Virginia Point," the hackman explained. "Best thing for me to do, when you get ready to cross, is to take you down to the mouth of Old River. There's always a lot of accomodation boats waiting there to take folks across San Jacinto Bay, or down to Galveston Island. It's a sight quicker to go that way, too, if you're in any kinda hurry."

"You know the town and I don't," Longarm said. "If you say that's the easiest way to get over to the island, why that's the way I'll go."

51

Leaning back on the leather seat, Longarm relaxed while the hackman maneuvered his vehicle away from the busy crisscross traffic that filled the street in front of the depot and started for the business section of the bustling town. It seemed to Longarm that he rode for a long time before the hack pulled up in front of a gleamingly new and imposing limestone structure with the legend UNITED STATES GOVERN-MENT arching in bronze letters above the door.

Inside, wide corridors branched off a spacious lobby. Signs at each of the hallways identified the offices located on each one, and Longarm had no trouble finding his way to the U.S. marshal's headquarters. Chief Marshal Pete Clanahan was an imposing figure of a man. He towered over Longarm by a half-head and his chest looked as broad as an elephant's. His dark-brown eyes were opaque, as though he purposely shielded them from giving away what he was thinking.

"How's Billy Vail making out up in Denver?" Clanahan asked after Longarm had introduced himself and had been invited into the chief marshal's private office.

"He's holding up pretty good," Longarm replied. "He sends you his regards."

"When he told you you were being sent down here, did he give you any hint why?" Clanahan frowned.

"Only that I'm looking for a missing Secret Service Agent."

"That's all I know myself," Clanahan said, his frown deepening. "They had me send one of my men to Florida, of all places, and didn't say please, thank you, or kiss my butt. I was hoping you'd know."

"Maybe when this investigation's finished, we'll all find out why we're supposed to be digging out old Trea-sury bonds for some damn foreign bank," Longarm told him. "But all I'm going to do is follow orders and see what comes out."

"That's all any of us can do," Clanahan agreed.

Longarm stood up, saying, "I ain't trying to cut my visit short, Chief Clanahan, but right now. I better get busy again. I'd like to get over to Galveston Island before it's too dark to see my way around."

"If you get in a tight jam and need a hand, be sure to let me know, Long."

"I'll do that," Longarm replied nodding.

"I'm always short of men, but I can scrape up help for one of our own if they get into some kind of jackpot," Clanahan went on, extending his hand to Longarm for a farewell handshake.

"I don't figure I'll need no help, but if I do, I'll get word to you by hook or crook," Longarm told him. "And if I get over here again, I'll stop by just to say hello."

Chapter 5

Walking along the shore of Buffalo Bayou, Longarm studied the small boats bobbing at the seemingly endless line
of short piers that jutted into the water. Though a bend in
the bayou's curving bank cut off his vision half a mile or
more upstream, as far as he could see small boats lined the
entire waterfront.

Even at the stretches between the wharves the little craft
were crowded close together along the riverbank, nosed
in to the shore for lack of a mooring spot. Beyond the
curve, he could see the masts of still more small sailboats
rising above the line of the horizon like oversized tooth-
picks that swayed and oscillated against the sky.

Most of the craft that were fully visible held a man,
sometimes two. Though a few of the boatmen were coiling
ropes or mending sails, most of them merely sat somno-
lent, staring across the greenish water of the bayou.

Except for the variances in their sizes, Longarm could
see very little difference between the little vessels. Almost
all of the smaller boats had stubby masts, and on the larger
craft the masts rose a dozen feet high, often higher. For
the most part the craft looked a bit shabby and unkempt,
though a few sparkled with shining fresh paint. Only one
out of every dozen or so of them boasted cabins, and the
smaller of the boats had no decks.

"You might just as well pick out one of 'em and get on with your business, old son," Longarm told himself as he stopped to light one of his long thin cigars. "Because it don't make no never-mind which one you hire to go over to Galveston Island in, since you ain't going to like crossing that big stretch of water."

Longarm walked a few steps farther along the bank and was about to make his choice by counting out the half-dozen boats nearest him in eeny-meeny-miney-moe fashion when voices were raised in angry shouts behind him. He turned to locate the source of the disturbance.

Just below him a man stood on the bank at the water's edge. He had an oar in his hands and was waving it like a club, his target a second man who stood almost knee-deep in the bayou's grey-green waters. The man in the water was obviously having trouble holding his footing on the sloping bottom. Slipping with almost every step he started to move parallel to the shore, but the one on the bank followed him. Each time the wading man turned and headed for dry land the one wielding the oar swung it threateningly.

Longarm's sympathy went at once to the underdog. Two giant strides down the slope brought him to the man with the oar. He grabbed the oar blade and yanked it away as he said, "I don't know what kinda fuss you and that fellow out there's having, but if you got something between you to settle, do it by fighting fair and square!"

"Who the hell asked you to butt in?" the other growled. "It ain't no business of yours!"

"Nobody did, but you're wrong about it not being any of my affair. Was that fellow out in the water to get drowned and I saw how you were responsible for it, I'd have to arrest you for murdering him. I just aimed to save all three of us from any more trouble. I don't—"

56

Longarm did not have a chance to finish what he'd started to say. The man in the water had lost no time in taking advantage of his opportunity to move without hindrance. As soon as he saw Longarm grab the oar he changed his course and started for the shore. He'd reached dry ground by the time Longarm was explaining to the oar wielder and made a beeline for them.

Grabbing his would-be assailant's collar he pulled the man around and swung a roundhouse blow at his jaw. The second man countered the punch in time to keep it from landing. Then the two squared off like a pair of banty roosters in a barnyard and began punching and counterpunching. Neither of them wasted breath in talking, and from the silent ferocity shown by both men Longarm realized at once that they were in a battle to the finish.

Only a few of the blows either man launched went to their intended marks, for the steeply slanted embankment was perhaps the world's worst spot for a fistfight. The two opponents were not equally matched, as the man who'd been wielding the oar stood almost a head taller than the other. However, the wet slick slanting ground equalized any odds that might have existed, for its treacherous footing prevented either of them from bracing his feet to loose really telling blows. Both men skidded and slipped and fewer than half the punches launched by either of them landed.

Having evened the odds, Longarm took no further part in whatever dispute had brought the battlers to their bout of fist slinging. He backed away from them and stood watching. None of the men in the boats nearby seemed inclined to interfere by joining the fracas or separating the fighters. They watched in silence and no cheers were raised for either of the combatants, who were circling and sparring, flailing the air with their fists, launching a blow when they saw an opportunity.

Only a few minutes after the fight had started both men had begun to breathe hard. The few yards of the riverbank over which they'd fought was growing more slippery as the combatants ranged back and forth. Longarm could see that the fight must end soon, but the climax came earlier than he'd expected. The man who'd started the fracas sensed or saw or felt that his adversary's blows were beginning to lose their steam. He braced himself for a fight-ending roundhouse punch, but without having taken the glance that was needed to check on his footing.

He swung from his hip level and the blow would indeed have ended the fight if it had landed, but in midswing his braced foot skidded on the wet bare soil. The strength that had been intended to add finishing force to the blow he was launching provided the momentum to start him skidding down the bank and into the water.

He hit with a splash and went under, surfaced and fought for footing. His feet could not find a solid spot on the bottom of the bayou, while the efforts he was making to stand up kept carrying him away from shore into the deeper water. He was almost shoulder-deep when he succeeded in stabilizing himself on a solid spot of the bottom.

He gave one glance at his adversary standing poised and waiting at the water's edge. When he saw that the other was ready, standing with fists in position to start swinging, he very obviously lost whatever desire he had to finish the fight. Half wading and half swimming, he started away, angling slowly for the shore at a spot that would be forty or fifty feet from the area where the fracas had been taking place.

Still wet, his clothing clinging to him in wrinkled puckers, the young man who'd came out winner turned to Longarm and said, "I owe you for giving me a chance to get back on shore."

"You don't owe me a blessed thing," Longarm replied. "I guess anybody'd have butted in and stopped him from murdering you right here in broad daylight."

"I could sure see that son of a bitch Ockerman had all the edge," the youth added. "He'd've killed me with his oar if you hadn't been around and stopped him."

"Ockerman's the name of the fellow you were fighting?"

"Yep. He'd've had a harder time than he was looking for before he killed me, though. I wasn't aiming to give up, but I guess I wouldn't't've made much of a show if it hadn't been for you, him with that oar and me bare-handed."

Longarm had been studying the young man while they talked. Despite his wet, muddy clothes and bare feet, the youth had a friendly manner. He looked to be in his early twenties, his face was deeply tanned and formed a sharp contrast to the shock of reddish-blond hair that frizzled below the flat-topped narrow-brimmed straw hat he had on. The streaks of mud that had spattered his face during his run-in still clung to the growth of sparse whiskers covering his cheeks and his squared jutting chin. He was a few days past the need for a shave, and the thin spatters of wet mud that clotted at the roots of each whisker gave him the appearance of having spread a polka-dot bandana over his face.

"Not that it's any of my business," Longarm commented, "and I ain't just being nosy about yours, but I sorta got the idea that you got a running fight going on with that fellow."

"I have, but I didn't go looking for it. It ain't all on my side. The thing is, I keep my boat nice and clean all the time, and Ockerman don't. Then when him and me has to moor our boats close together while we wait for customers to show up, most people pick my boat instead of his."

"And that's all you're fighting over?"

"It's enough. There's been more boats than passengers of late, and customers are worth fighting over."

"Well, I can see how that'd come about," Longarm said. "But while we're talking about hiring boats, that's what I'm down here at the bayou for."

"If you're hiring, I'll be proud to have your trade."

"I sorta figured you might be interested, looking at all the boats that I see waiting up and down along the bank here."

"It's sorta slow right now," the youth admitted. "But I'm going to tell you right out that if you're figuring to do any kind of smuggling from some ship offshore, I'm not interested, even if a lot of these other boatmen are."

"I'm no smuggler," Longarm assured him. "I'm just looking for someone who knows the lay of the land hereabouts, and you look like you do."

"Sure I do. I know the water and I know the coastline. I can take you anyplace bigger boats could and some places where they can't."

"You might tell me how much you charge when you hire out," Longarm suggested.

"I get two dollars a day, sunup to sundown, and an extra dollar at night, when it's tougher getting around out there on the bay. You furnish your own victuals. And I don't see that you've got any fishing tackle along, so if you want to rent some from me—"

"Fishing ain't what I got in mind," Longarm broke in, then smiled and amended his remark. "Leastways, not the same kind of fishing your other customers are interested in doing."

60

"Whatever you're interested in doing doesn't bother me, as long as it don't break the law, mister."

"Now, that's a right good answer. Let's talk a little bit more and get sorta acquainted before I tell you what I got in mind." Longarm extended his hand as he added, "First off, my name's Long, Custis Long."

"Pleased to meet you, Mr. Long. I'm Tom"—he pronounced his name as though it was spelled T-a-w-m—"Saunders. And I'd be glad to hire out to you."

"You might not be so glad when I tell you that I'm a deputy United States marshal."

"That don't worry me a smidgen, Marshal Long. If I've broke any laws, I don't know what they'd be."

"Oh, I didn't come down here to the bayou looking for you, or anybody else in particular. I work outa the Denver office, and I was sent here on a case that don't have a thing to do with boats or fishing or anything like that. But I do need to do some poking around, here and over on Galveston Island, and I don't know beans about boats."

"I wouldn't want to get crossways of any smugglers," the young man admitted. "They've got some real mean ways of treating folks who tip off the coast patrol about what they're up to."

Longarm shook his head. "I don't have anything to do with the coast patrol. And smugglers are the last thing I'm worried about, unless they get in the way of my job. Now, if you want my business—"

"Oh, I want it all right," young Saunders broke in. "And what's more, I need it. I can start soon, if you're in a hurry to get over to Galveston Island."

"Well, I want to go there first-off," Longarm informed him. "So the sooner I can get started, the better. But I didn't know how long it might take me to hire a boat and all like that. I just came down here to take a look around. I'd need to go back to town and get some things. How long does it take to get over to the island, anyway?''

''If this wind holds from the shore, it'll take five or six hours. But it'll be longer if we're bucking a fresh blow from the gulf.''

Longarm was silent for a moment, an idea forming in his head. He said, ''You just mentioned that you don't mind sailing at night, and I'd imagine you'll have a few chores to do before you're ready to go.''

''That's right. They're all little jobs, like filling the water jug and bending on an extra foresail that I might need tonight if the wind changes.''

''How'd it strike you to take care of what-all you got to do while I got into town? Then we'll set out soon as I get back.''

''That'd likely put us into the Galveston harbor about daybreak.'' Tom Saunders said after a moment of thoughtful silence. ''Unless we run into some crosswinds. But I better tell you before we close any kind of deal, my boat hasn't got a cabin for you to sleep in. The best I can do for a bed is fold up a spare sail in the bottom of the boat.''

''That won't make no never-mind,'' Longarm assured him. ''I'm used to sleeping just about anyplace.''

''I haven't got a galley, either, so I can't serve up hot food.''

''I carry some jerky and parched corn in my saddlebags. It'll do me.''

''Then as long as you know what you can look for, I'll be right glad to make a deal with you.''

''Far as I'm concerned, we got one right now,'' Longarm said. He fished a gold double-eagle out of his pocket and handed it to young Saunders. ''That'll pay for a couple of nights with some left over. It's likely I'll owe you more later on, but that'll depend on how this case shapes up. You keep track of however big a bill I run up, and we'll settle our account when I get my case closed.''

Longarm's cases had taken him out in boats on bays and lakes before, but he had never sailed on a body of water under a sky that was dark, yet still seemed to emit light. The sky over Galveston Bay was a deep midnight blue and the surface of the water was pitch-black. The myriad stars that filled the sky gave no real illumination, but created a sort of diffused glow that was refracted from both the sky and the water.

Although he could not see anything except black night-sky and stars twenty or thirty feet in the darkness that stretched beyond the boat's rail, by the starshine he could make out a fair amount of detail in the little single-masted craft itself. He could follow the seams in the high triangular sail halfway to its tip, and he had no trouble seeing the ropes coiled along the boat's rail and the dunnage spread here and there on the sloping deck.

Longarm was sitting just past the center of the little craft, on the small square shelf made by the heavy timbers in which the vessel's mast was stepped. The bags and bundles that lay on the bottom and Tom Saunders's face at the tiller in the stern were almost as plainly visible as they had been during the final minutes of daylight when they'd pulled away for the mooring on the bank of Buffalo Bayou and entered the bay itself.

''If it don't get in the way of thinking about what-all you got to do, I got a few questions about Galveston Island that' I'd like to ask you,'' he told Tom.

''Ask away, Marshal Long. I won't promise that I can answer all of 'em, but I'll try.''

63

"That island's a place I haven't been to for a while. From what I gather, it's settled up pretty good."

"Well, Galveston City's got maybe ten thousand people living in it, but most of them's rich people that thinks they're a cut above us common folks. We got our own sorta town over on Pelican Island."

"Now, I never heard about Pelican Island," Longarm told his companion, frowning with puzzlement.

"It ain't much of a place, I guess. Sorta a shantytown, like Houston was till a few years ago. A lot of 'em's Mescins that come here when Mexico owned everything clear to the Mississippi River."

"That was quite a stretch back," Longarm countered.

"Not to hear some of the others tell it, the ones that claim to've settled on Galveston Island before the Mescins got there. They say they was living there when Jean Lafitte taken it over for his pirates."

"Why, that was even longer ago!"

"By quite a few years," Saunders agreed. "But them rich nabobs that lives in Galveston City, they don't mix much with anybody that ain't their own kind."

"What about the rest of the folks?"

"Oh, most of 'em are Johnny-come-latelies like me. A lot of them moved away during the war, when the Confederates taken things over, but that was when my folks come there."

"How in tunket do they all make a living on a little island like that?" Longarm kept his face expressionless when he asked the question he'd been leading up to.

"Why, there's stores and a hotel and a lot of saloons and a few little-bitty farms. And a whole passel of fishing boats make Galveston City their home ports because the best catches come outa the gulf beyond the island."

64

"And there's a lot of boats, you say?"

"Maybe more than you seen along Buffalo Bayou. Leaving from the island they save a lot of time when they go out seining."

"I guess they can sell just about all they catch?"

"Oh, sure. The railroads all got ice cars now, and what don't go to the markets in Houston they ship on out. And some of the fisherman don't use nets, they troll for sharks."

"What in tunket do they do with them big ugly things?"

"Sell their skins and livers. They're worth a lot of money."

"Well, I'll get along without 'em," Longarm said. "I don't guess there's any pirates left?"

"Some of the landfolks claims there is. I've heard a lot of stories about pirates on Pelican Island, but my daddy always said I was to mind my own affairs, so I don't go poking my nose into things that ain't none of my business."

A frown had grown on Longarm's face while Tom was talking. He asked, "Where in tunket's Pelican Island at? I don't recall that I ever heard of it before."

"Most folks haven't. It's just a big rock all covered with birdshit and pelican nests. There ain't really what you'd call a town on it, just houses all scattered out."

"I guess we'll be going by it, so you can show it—" Longarm stopped short when the booming report of a gunshot broke the stillness. A brief flash of muzzle blast broke the distant darkness and dozens of small fountains of water rose white around the boat as pellets from the gun splashed into the dark water. Several of the pellets hit the gunwales with small angry spatting noises.

"Get down behind the gunnels!" Saunders exclaimed. "That's a goose gun shooting, someplace off our stern!"

Longarm was already dropping to the bottom of the boat.

He saw the red flash of another shot brighten the night sky and a second series of splashes came from the disturbed water. Again a few pellets rattled against the sturdy oak gunwales.

By this time Longarm had crawled the short distance to his Winchester, which was lying across his saddlebags. He pulled it from its scabbard and rose to his knees, levering a shell into the chamber as he shouldered the rifle.

"You can't do any good with a rifle in the dark!" Saunders protested.

"When anybody shoots at me, I shoot back," Longarm snapped without raising his head from the rifle's sights. He did not take the time needed to explain to young Saunders that this was far from being the first time he'd exchanged shots in the dark with unseen adversaries, and that he'd honed his marksmanship to the sharpness of a razor's edge in responding to the shooting of hidden outlaws.

As a third burst of reddish light broke the night, Longarm triggered off a shot in its general direction before the muzzle blast from their attacker's gun died away and still another shower of lead pellets beat a light tattoo on the boat's side.

Without changing his point of aim, Longarm got off two more fast shots. Hard on the heels of the second shot the sound of splintering wood reached their ears, and again red muzzle blast broke the blackness a hundred yards or more away and the flat roaring rumble of the goose gun broke the silence. This time the dark surface of the gently heaving water only a half dozen yards away was pocked with white bubbles in a dozen places.

"They're shooting short, but that last chunk of lead I sent at 'em sure as hell hit something solid," Longarm said. He kept the rifle shouldered and ready, but no more red muzzle blasts broke the darkness to provide him with even the suggestion of a target.

For the next few minutes they waited in the gently rocking boat for a glimpse of the mysterious vessel that had attacked them, or for the men aboard it to fire the goose gun again. No more shots broke the night's blackness, and no sounds except the waves broke the silence.

"Was you to ask me, I'd say whoever done that shooting's give up and gone," Longarm said at last.

"I figure so, too," Tom answered. "And I guess we both know who it was. That damn Ockerman followed us outa Buffalo Bayou and hung back till dark before he tried to get even. He might've got me, too, if it hadn't been for you being along with that rifle."

"You might just be right about who it was, Tom," Longarm said. "Except I don't see how you could prove it in a court of law."

"Oh, I know that, Marshal Long. But there'll be a time when we'll be face-to-face again, and I'll get even then. But I better get busy and check our course. I want to be sure to get you right up to the Galveston pier."

"Now, that's something I can't help you with, so I'm going to stretch out on the sail and catch forty winks. I got a passel of getting around to do, come daylight, and I don't aim to start out tired."

Longarm suited his actions to his words. He stretched out on the folds of canvas and in a few minutes was sleeping soundly.

Chapter 6

"It's too bad we had to tack back all this way," Tom apologized as he gave a final tightening tug to the mooring rope. "But you saw how it was all along the shore, not a place where we could tie up at any of the docks."

"Don't fash yourself about it, Tom," Longarm said. "I got a lot better idea now than I had about how the land lays."

"We're going to have a long walk back to the café, though," Tom pointed out.

"That don't make no never-mind," Longarm told the young boatman. "I guess my rifle and gear's going to be safe if I leave everything on your boat?"

"Nobody around here steals. If they do, they don't last long."

"Then again, my rifle just might come in handy," Longarm remarked as he stepped up from the boat to the dock. "To tell you the truth, I need a little bit of a walk to get the kinks outa my legs after curling around in the bottom of your boat last night. Boats are all right, but they sure ain't got much room for a man to stretch out his legs in."

Standing on the pier in the fresh salt-laden air, Longarm looked at the line of buildings that filled the street facing the wharves. Beyond them he could see the slate and shingle roofs of houses, and where the two- and three-story business buildings did not block the view to the east he could get glimpses of imposing brick and cut-stone residences.

Longarm shook his head as he went on, "I've been here to Galveston before, and it never does look much like a Texas town to me. Looks more like it belongs back East, where all of them rich, high-society muckety-mucks live."

"Well, I wouldn't know about that, because I never had a chance to go east," Tom told him. "I was born here, but that was after the war was over, so I don't know what it used to be like. But I've heard old folks talk a lot about how it used to be on the island here, and how things have changed since the rich people started moving to the east end of it after the war."

"It didn't used to be all spread out like it is now."

"Not from what I've heard." Tom pointed to the west along the waterfront where other, less imposing buildings made a jagged line facing the bay. "That's where the town began. It's pretty much gone to seed now, but there's one restaurant down there called Donovan's. I've heard it's one of Mort Clouter's places, but it's one café here where we'll get a good hot breakfast cheap."

"Who's Mort Clouter?" Longarm frowned.

"He's supposed to be the boss of all the crooks on Galveston Island and the man that's behind the gambling games in all the saloons. I don't know him myself, but I suppose what's said about him's the truth."

Longarm nodded. "I know his kind. But if this place you mentioned puts out a good breakfast, I don't see why we hadn't ought to go there."

"I thought maybe because you're on the side of the law—" Tom began.

"If he owns that place you was just talking about, it ain't no skin off of my nose," Longarm said. "And them few little bites we had last night has all wore off by now. Besides, you know this town better than I do."

"I don't know the new part, where all the swells live now," Tom replied. "But I know my way around the waterfront. Not that there's a lot of it to know. There's only three or four streets that amount to anything back from the bay. And where we're heading on this street we're on now it's mostly a string of saloons and whorehouses and rooming houses for sailors and dock wallopers."

"Sounds like a lot of other places I've been," Longarm said. "But I ain't all that choosy. I'll settle for what we can get to eat at this place we're heading for."

"Well, it's where us fisherman go to eat when we've got to have a meal in Galveston. The new part of town's too nabobby for folks like us. There's only one thing, though. I better—" Tom stopped short and a frown formed on his face as he looked at Longarm. He started to continue, thought better of it and shook his head.

"Go on and finish what you were starting to say," Longarm told him.

"I—I don't rightly know how to put this, Marshal Long," Tom began. He hesitated briefly, then went on, "What I think I oughta tell you is, there's some pretty rough characters that eat where we're going. I think, well—"

Longarm had faced similar situations before. He said, "I got a pretty good idea what you're getting at, Tom. You figure we might not be real welcome if your friends know I'm a lawman."

An expression of relief flashed onto the youth's face as

71

he nodded and said, "That's what I had in mind, all right."

"It ain't such a much of a thing. You're still being polite and I been calling you Tom all along. Now, I got a sorta nickname that a lot of folks call me by, and you're welcome to do the same. It's Longarm."

"Longarm?" Tom frowned, then the frown became a small smile as he said, "Sure. As far back as I can remember right up to the day he died, I've heard my daddy say he'd like to see the long arm of the law stretch far enough to reach over here to Galveston Island and gather up all the crooks."

"From what you've sorta hinted around and what the chief in the U.S. marshal's office in Houston told me, that's a job I'd hate to take on," Longarm said. "But now that we got the name business settled, let's go find that café you told me about and get some breakfast."

As he and Tom walked along the waterfront, the rising sun at their backs now, Longarm could see the difference between the part of Galveston they were leaving and the area ahead of them. Desertion rather than the ravages of time appeared to him to be the main reason for the shabby looks of the broken line of buildings they passed as they walked slowly along the waterfront.

For every building that showed evidence of constant care, there were three or four from which the paint had peeled in great patches, exposing the surface of raw red brick or brown adobe or wide weather-tanned boards. Only the few cut-stone buildings gave an effect of uniform neatness. The doors and windows of some of the houses had been boarded over, and in the walls of those whose owners had neglected to take this precaution the glass windowpanes had been shattered by weather or by vandals looking for loot.

In contrast to the neglected structures, the fronts of the few buildings which had been cared for gleamed like jewels in a morass of mud. Even the cut-stone structures which had boarded doors and windows appeared neat. The majority of windows in the houses that gave evidence of continued occupancy gleamed in the slanting rays of the morning sun, which was bright enough almost to obscure the red-shaded lamps that glowed behind lace-curtained windows. Many of the other houses had been fitted with the swinging doors which marked them as saloons, and though at this early hour the waterfront street was deserted, lights showed above and below the entrance doors.

Longarm stopped suddenly when he caught sight of a brass plate on one of the less shabby buildings they were passing. He took a second look at the front of the white limestone structure. It was one of the neater buildings, and a frown grew on his face as he reread the legend that appeared on the verdigris-spotted brass sign: BARCLAY'S BANK, LTD — GALVESTON BRANCH.

Tom had halted beside Longarm. He asked, "What's wrong, Longarm?"

"I'm wondering about the building over yonder with that sign on it," Longarm replied, pointing. "You happen to know if it's still a bank?"

"Why, if the sign says it's a bank, I reckon it is," Tom said. "I've seen the door open when I passed by, but I never paid much mind to it. You know, Longarm, us fisherman don't do a lot of business with banks. Most of the time we don't even have enough money to weight our pockets much."

"Sure"—Longarm nodded—"I got that same trouble

73

myself. But even if it is a bank, it's too early for it to be open. After breakfast we'll stop back by here and I'll see what I can find out."

They moved along, and after they'd passed another dozen or so old dwellings that had been converted to saloons or red-light establishments, Tom pointed to the largest of the houses that remained ahead.

"That's Donovan's, the big house yonder," he said.

"And we ain't going to get there a minute too soon to suit me," Longarm told him. "My belly's been cutting up didoes for the last few minutes. It's yelling for grub so loud you can damn near hear it. I guess a man can get a drink of rye whiskey there too, if he asks, can't he?"

"Oh, sure. Half of the downstairs is a saloon, the other half's the restaurant."

"Then let's go in by the saloon door. It'll only take a minute for us to put away a swallow of rye."

"You can have my share of whiskey, Longarm," Tom said. "I don't drink anything stronger than beer."

"You have whatever you want," Longarm told him, "But I'll stick with rye. It helps me set up my appetite— not that I need anything to do that now. Anyways, soon as we've lifted our elbows, we'll be ready for a big platter of ham and eggs."

There was only one difference between the saloon they entered and others where Longarm had bellied up to the bar in the many towns where his cases had taken him. The difference was the big arched doorway in one side wall that led into the dining room. Through it they could see most of the long counter that spanned one side, and the dozen or so small tables that crowded the floor. Longarm stepped up to the bar and dropped a half-dollar on it.

74

Before the ringing of the coin had died away, an aproned barkeep was in front of him.

"Beer for my friend here and rye for me," Longarm said. "Maryland rye, Tom Moore, if you got any. If you ain't, I guess I'll have to settle for whatever you pour."

"Just happens we've got Tom Moore," the man replied after turning to look at the backbar, where bottles lined three tiers of shelves between the mirrored walls. "But all the bottles on them backbar shelves is special prime whiskey that costs extra."

"Go ahead and pour a shot for me," Longarm told him. "Whatever it costs, it's worth the extra to get a decent drink."

Taking a bottle from one of the backbar shelves the barkeep set it with a glass in front of Longarm, but instead of filling the shot glass, he moved to the nearest beer spigot and filled a stein, which he shoved across the mahogany to Tom. He made no move to pick up the coin that Longarm had placed on the bar.

Tom picked up his stein of beer and said, "Thanks for the beer, Longarm. But I'm a lot hungrier than I am thirsty. You come on over to the café side when you've had your drink. I'm going to take my beer and go see if I can get us a table where we can talk a little more private than at the counter."

"You do that," Longarm said. "And if the waiter comes around before I get there, just order me a big plate of ham and eggs and some hot biscuits."

Longarm waited, sipping his whiskey, until the barkeep had passed by twice, serving patrons on either side of him. Then he shoved the half-dollar toward the man and said, "You better pick this up, friend, before I leave and somebody sneaks it into his own pocket."

"I wasn't forgetting it," the aproned barkeep replied. "I was waiting for you to pay the half-dollar you owe the house for the other drink."

"What other drink?" Longarm frowned. "All I had was one shot of that Tom Moore."

"Maybe you didn't think I was looking, but after you downed the shot I poured you, I saw you tip the bottle for another one. But I'll tell you what I'll do. You pay up for two drinks and I'll throw in the beer on the house."

Longarm said nothing for a moment. He'd encountered crooked bartenders before, those like Denver's legendary Harry Tammen, who tossed each silver dollar or half-dollar he was paid for a drink up to the saloon's ceiling. If the coin stuck, Tammen passed it on to the bar's owner, but if the money fell back on the mahogany he put it into his own pocket.

Unless he felt justified in bending the truth in order to trap a lawbreaker, any crookedness or cheating, no matter how small, ruffled Longarm's lawman instinct. He locked eyes with the barkeep and said, "I had just one drink outa that Tom Moore bottle. If you want a dime for the beer, say so."

"I want another half-dollar for the shot of that rye whiskey you poured yourself when you thought I wasn't looking!" the bartender insisted.

"There's two things I ain't got no use for," Longarm told the man. "And I guess you can figure out what they are. Now, suppose we just let it go at that and not swap no hard words."

Leaving the half-dollar on the bar, Longarm walked away and joined Tom Saunders in the crowded restaurant. He was a bit surprised when he saw the youth sitting at a

76

table with someone else. He stopped behind the stranger just as Tom looked up.

"Longarm, I want you to meet a friend of mine," Tom said. Longarm stepped around, and as the stranger turned to face him, he concealed his surprise when he saw that Tom's companion was a woman. Tom went on, "This is Topacia Trechas," He turned to the woman and said, "Longarm's the fellow I was just starting to tell you about, Topacia. He took up for me when that Clee Ockerman started getting nasty up in Buffalo Bayou."

"I'm pleased," she said, extending her hand. Longarm hid his astonishment again when Topacia stood up to shake hands and he felt the steel-like hardness of her palm and fingers.

"Topacia's as good at fishing as any man you'll find along the Gulf Coast," Tom went on. "She was just asking me if I'd be her partner today in a two-boat trawl, and I haven't told her yes or no yet. I didn't want to say for sure until I could find out if you're going to need me any more till evening."

While Tom was talking Longarm had been covertly examining Topacia. She was almost as tall as he was, but he could tell nothing more than her height because the loose heavy canvas jacket above the jeans she wore concealed her figure. Her eyes were midnight black, her eyebrows and lashes thick, her nose a straight line from her brow to her full red lips. She had high cheekbones and a firm rounded chin, and like Tom, her skin bore the deep tan of one who was constantly exposed to the Gulf Coast's steady sunshine.

"I'm pleased to meet you, Longarm," she said. Her voice was throaty, almost hoarse. "I didn't know Tom had chartered to you when I asked him to trawl with me."

77

"I won't throw no monkey wrenches," Longarm told her. "But it looks right now like I got a full day's work here on shore, doing some jobs that Tom can't help me with. If you two can make a good haul, go at it."

"We'll go out as soon as we finish breakfast, then," Tom said. "And we'll be back in by sundown. After the sun's off the water the fish begin coming up close to the surface. A deep troll this near the shore toward evening won't bring up enough to make it worthwhile."

"That oughta give me all the time I need, then," Longarm said. As they sat down, Topacia between him and Tom, he went on, "Now, let's see if we can't get that waiter to bring us some grub. I'm about half starved."

"I put your order in along with mine," Tom said. "That was just before Topacia got here."

"I've eaten," she volunteered. "But I'll drink coffee with you, unless you've got private business to talk about."

"Join us and be welcome," Longarm invited. "Me and Tom won't have a lot to talk about until later."

Before they were seated, the waiter appeared with platters of ham and eggs and fried potatoes for Longarm and Tom. He served them and Longarm pitched in hungrily, as did Tom, while Topacia sipped coffee.

Tom was still eating when Longarm finished his own breakfast and pushed his plate away. He pulled his coffee cup in front of him, fished out one of his long thin cigars and was taking a match from his vest pocket when Topacia produced a shorter cigar that was as thin as his. She slid it between her lips. Longarm scratched the match into flame and held it for Topacia to light her cigar, then puffed his own into life.

"I hope you aren't too surprised, and don't object to my cigar habit," Topacia said as she took the small cigar from her lips. "But I picked it up from my husband when we were fishing together."

"I wouldn't make no objection to just about anything a lady that looks and talks as nice as you would want to do," Longarm told her. "And I don't imagine your husband made much of a fuss, either, when you decided you wanted to take up cigar smoking."

"Joaquim was happy to have me join him," she replied. "And I think of him each time I light a cigar, for he is no longer alive."

"Well, I'm real sorry to hear that," Longarm said.

"He has been dead long enough for me to overcome grief," she said, shrugging. "I think of him now and then, but life must still be lived in spite of sorrow."

"Joaquim was a good man," Tom put in. "And a good fisherman. I learned a lot from him when I was starting out."

"Yes, Joaquim was a better teacher of all things than I could be," Topacia explained. "He also taught me to fish, but one day he did what he always warned me not to do. He wrapped his handline too tightly around his palm. I think it must have been a shark that pulled him overboard. He went under and did not return."

"So you just stayed here and kept on fishing?" Longarm asked.

"Of course." Topacia's voice showed her surprise, then she went on, "I have been here too many years to leave. And it does me no embarrassment to say that I could not afford the steamer fare to return to Portugal. Besides, no one is left there now of my family, so I had no reason to return."

"Well, now, I'd say that making up your mind that way does you a lot of credit," Longarm told her.

"It does in my book," Tom observed. "And Topacia's as good at fishing as any man along the gulf." He stood up and turned to her. "But we'd better be putting out if we expect to bring in a payload today."

"You are right." She nodded, getting to her feet. She looked at Longarm and added, "It is pleasant to have met you. We will see one another again, I'm sure, if you are to be here on the island very long."

"I imagine I'll be around for a few days," he replied. "At least till I settle up the business that's brought me here."

Longarm watched Tom and Topacia leave, then settled back to finish his coffee and his cheroot. He turned his thoughts to the next move which he hoped would carry his case another step forward. By the time his coffee cup was empty and his cigar smoked to the butt he'd reached a decision.

Leaving the restaurant he retraced his way along the waterfront until he reached the building where he'd seen the brass plate carrying the Barclay Bank's name. The door stood ajar now. Stepping up to it, Longarm rapped. A long moment passed while the sound of papers being shuffled came through the crack between the door and its frame, then footsteps sounded inside and the door was pulled fully open.

"I guess this is the right place for me to come to, ain't it?" Longarm asked the man who stood facing him.

Even before Longarm spoke the thought flashed through his mind that the man looked like anything but a banker. He had the hulking broad-shouldered frame of a wrestler and the lumpy jaws and scarred face of a saloon brawler.

"Depends on what you come for," the man said. His thin high-pitched voice did not match his size and appearance.

"A fellow downtown told me this was the place I could cash in a paper I found and get real money for it," Longarm went on.

"What kind of paper?"

"Well, when I showed it to this fellow he said it was a bond put out by Barclay's Bank during the war. He said it's still good, even if it's old as it is, and it didn't make no difference because the South had lost."

"How'd you come by this piece of paper?"

"Now, I sure ain't going to tell nobody that," Longarm answered. "Because there might be some more where this one came from, and I'm the only one that knows where that is."

This time the man in the doorway did not hesitate. Opening the door wide as he spoke, he told Longarm, "I guess you better come on in. From what you said, I got a hunch the boss just might be interested in talking to you."

Chapter 7

Longarm did not stop to debate his next move. He stepped through the opened door into a long hallway. A quick glance to the left and another to the right was all that he had time for as he followed the man leading the way. The hall was a long one and as far as he could tell the barren corridor spanned the width of the building. There was no time for him to stop and explore it with his eyes, for the man ahead was going through a second door that stood in line with the entranceway. He was looking over his shoulder to make sure that Longarm was following.

Passing through the second door Longarm found himself in a wide rectangular room. His first impression was that the room saw little use, for it was not carpeted and at each step taken by him and the man ahead small puffs of fine dust rose from the wide board floor. He could tell that the room extended across the full width of the building, for it had doors at each end which stood ajar, and through them he got a glimpse of the hallway's extension and could see high barred windows in the outer wall.

His eyes swiveled busily as Longarm followed his guide across the room. Rough-hewn, exposed ceiling beams, unpainted and darkened by time, supported equally darkened planks that formed the ceiling. There was no chandelier suspended from the ceiling, but sconces on the walls held candles.

For all the spaciousness of the chamber, it was very sparsely furnished. A small table stood at each end under high barred windows, and four or five chairs were scattered at random on the floor. Three closed doors broke the rear wall.

Longarm halted a half step behind his guide when the man stopped in front of the center door and rapped. There was no response to the knocks for several moments, then the door was opened a small crack and from the room beyond a man asked, "What d'you want, Sid?"

"There's a fellow out here's asking about the bonds," Sid replied.

"Who is he?"

"Damned if I know, Mort. Big man. Sorta husky. Got a .45 Colt holstered on his hip and a Winchester in his hand."

"Has he got a name?" the man behind the door asked.

"I guess so. He didn't say what it is, though."

"Ask him, you damn fool!"

Turning to Longarm, the man addressed as Sid by the unknown asked, "What's your name?"

Longarm had been waiting for the question and had the answer ready. He said, "Custis."

Turning back to the barely open door, Sid reported, "He says his—"

"I heard what he said!" the invisible inquisitor broke in impatiently. "And I never heard the name Custis before. Find out who sent him."

Longarm had decided after the last exchange of second-hand questions that the time had come to get down to business. Before his escort could reply, he raised his voice and said, "I ain't got no idea who you are in there, or why you got to be so all-fired nosy about my name and all, without even coming in here and asking me yourself. Now, if you don't want to come out and talk to me man to man, I'll take my questions and my bonds someplace else."

For a long minute there was no reply from the man behind the door. Then it swung open and the speaker stepped into the room. Longarm saw a tall man with a sweeping mustache and thick beetling eyebrows. Both were snow-white, and so was his hair. He stopped just past the doorway, his face expressionless, his almost colorless eyes scanning Longarm with quick flickering movements that missed nothing.

Longarm had seen eyes like that before. In every case they had been in the face of a merciless killer. Now, he needed a second look to see the wrinkles on the newcomer's brow and cheeks and the neck wattles that gave further proof of his age. Then he transferred his attention to the man's clothing, a black frock coat and cream-colored trousers, the edges of a black-and-white checkered vest showing behind the wide lapels of the coat.

"Who told you to come here, Custis?" he asked at last.

"Why, there ain't nobody here in Galveston that tells me where I got to go or what to do," Longarm replied mildly. "A man that gets around any at all hears a lot of talk. If he's half smart, he disremembers a lot of the things he's heard."

"Who'd you hear talking about this place?"

"If I heard anybody talking about it, I disremember who it was. But I'd be a fool if I didn't tell you what I came in here for. It just so happens that I got a big bump of curiosity, and I got curious about that sign you got outside. This place don't look like no bank to me."

85

"Never mind what it looks like," the man retorted. "And don't worry about the sign. If you've come here to do any kind of business, let's get down to it."

"There's times when I'll do business with almost anybody that I run into," Longarm said. "And there's times when I even go out looking for somebody to do business with. And there's times when I ain't inclined to do business with anybody. I still ain't made up my mind about doing any with you, mister."

While he talked, he was sliding one of his long thin cigars out of his pocket. Without taking his eyes off the man in the doorway he fumbled in his vest pocket for a match and flicked a thumbnail over the match head. His eyes still studying the newcomer, Longarm puffed the tip of his cheroot into a red glow and exhaled a cloud of smoke.

As the smoke curled and drifted away, Longarm went on, "But them is times when I ain't got a lot of money riding on a blind hand."

"You're new in Galveston," the man in the doorway announced. "I know I've never seen your face before, any more than I've heard the name Custis."

"You make a pretty fair guess, mister," Longarm replied. "But I never heard the name Mort tossed around, neither."

For a moment a shadow of doubt flickered in the man's eyes, then he realized that Longarm had heard the man who'd opened the door calling him. The shadow vanished and he said, "Try Mort Clouter."

As soon as he'd heard the name, Longarm recalled that Tom had mentioned Mort Clouter as the man in control of Galveston's criminal element. He realized that he now had a major decision to make and quickly decided that even if the hunch he felt was wrong, he'd risk it. He shook his head and said, "I guess it's on account of I'm new in town, but the name don't ring no bells for me."

"Then why the hell are you bothering me, busting in this way?" Clouter demanded.

"I already told you that. I seen the bank sign outside."

"If it's Barclay's Bank you're looking for, they moved over across the bay to Houston. That was fifteen, maybe twenty years ago. If you knew anything about Barclay's, you sure as hell ought to know that."

"I'm a stranger in these parts," Longarm told Clouter, glad to be back on truthful ground for a change, "Hell, I came through Houston on my way here and I never even stopped to look around none. I just figured—"

Clouter broke in, "You just figured that Barclay's Bank here in Galveston issued some bonds a long time ago, during the war between the North and South. Someplace by hook or crook you picked up one of the bonds and found out that this was the place to come to cash it in. Now, isn't that the way of it?"

"Seems to me you know all about it," Longarm replied. "If you do, what's the need of all these questions you're plaguing me with?"

"Just go ahead and answer 'em," Clouter snapped.

Longarm was now playing the impromptu role he'd been forced into when he took the chance of entering unknown territory in search of a clue. He studied Clouter while taking his time replying. At last he replied to Clouter's question with a query of his own.

"Well, now, suppose it is. There ain't nothing wrong about what I'm after, not that I know of."

"I didn't say there was. Mind telling me where you've come from?"

"No reason why not," Longarm answered. "I come here outa Denver."

"Were you there a good while, or just passing through?"

"I've spent enough time there to get acquainted with a few folks."

"Know a fellow called George Law?"

George Law was not a strange name to Longarm, as he'd run into it while investigating a mail coach robbery which Law had been suspected of committing. He replied, "I don't to say I know him, but I've heard his name called a time or two."

"How about Joe Antrim?"

Clouter's earlier questions had given Longarm the clue to the reason for his quizzing. Only a man who belonged to the shadowy and ever-shifting outlaw fraternity would be likely to know the real name of Billy the Kid's half-brother, or that of a wanted man like Law.

Choosing his words carefully, he said, "Seems to me there used to be a faro dealer in Denver who called himself that. For all I know, he's still there. I can't say I know him. I'm a poker player myself."

"You ever work a table?" Clouter asked next. "Dealer? Stick-man? Spinner?"

Longarm shook his head. "Gambling ain't my line. I only work at jobs like them now and then, when I got to."

"I guess you know how to use that Colt you're packing?"

"I've had to use it a time or two. You can see I'm still walking around."

At last Clouter seemed satisfied. He nodded, then turned to the man who'd admitted Longarm and said, "Go on back to whatever it was you were doing when you let Custis in, Sid." Without waiting to see what Sid did, he faced Longarm and went on, "Come on into my office with me, Custis. Even if I don't know you from Adam's off-ox, I can always use a man like you seem to be from what you've been saying.''

Clouter's office was as impersonal and as sparsely furnished as the big room. The office had no windows. Its walls were unadorned, the floor uncarpeted. It's furniture consisted of a rectangular oak table that took up most of the center floorspace, a half dozen chairs along the walls, and in one corner an imposingly large safe. Clouter gestured to the chairs.

''Pull up a chair and sit down, Custis,'' he said as he moved around to the chair behind the table and settled into it.

Longarm pulled a chair up to the table and sat down a bit gingerly. His cigar had gone out during the long give-and-take with Clouter, and he relighted it. He blew out the match and let it fall to the floor, then looked across the table at Clouter.

''When I was asking you all those questions, I wasn't just being curious,'' Clouter began.

''I didn't figure you was,'' Longarm said, nodding.

''You had the answers I was looking for,'' Clouter went on. ''I'd say you know a little bit about me, or you wouldn't've come here. Have you really got one of those Confederate bonds, or was that just a bluff to get in here?''

''Oh, I got the bond, all right. I ain't going to say how I come by it, or when or where or for what, because that's my own business.''

''Don't worry. You've given me all the answers I need on that, and we can talk about you cashing it in later on,'' Clouter told him. ''What I want to know right now is, being that you're a stranger here in Galveston, how'd you find out about me?''

"I listen a lot," Longarm replied. "Just like I'm listening to you right now. When I've heard what you've got to say, I'll make up my mind what I want to do."

"You're sort of an independent cuss, too, aren't you?"

"I guess you could say that." Longarm nodded, then went on, being equally truthful, "But if I take on a job, I aim to finish it or know the reason why I can't."

"And you're as close-mouthed as you are independent." Clouter smiled a wolfish grin. "Tell me something else, Custis. How many Wanted circulars are out on you?"

"Now, that's something I don't talk about," Longarm answered unhesitatingly and again truthfully added, "but I'll guarantee you won't find none on me here in Texas."

Clouter nodded and said, "I had an idea that'd be the case. Which is a pretty good recommendation for a job with me."

"I don't recall saying I was looking for a job that'd need any kinda recommendation."

"Would you turn down one, if the money's right?"

"Are you offering?"

"That depends. Are you of a mind to listen if I did make you an offer?"

"That'd depend on the job. And the money."

"What would you say if I told you I've been thinking about spreading out my territory and opening up in Houston? It hasn't been worth much until now, but all of a sudden it's getting to be a big place."

"I could see that when I came through it," Longarm said with a nod. "But I was sorta figuring on taking life easy for a while. A hundred thousand dollars is a pretty good stack to lean back on."

"I can tell that you don't know all there is to know about those Confederate bonds, Custis." Clouter smiled.

It was the sort of smug smile that Longarm had seen on the face of greenhorns at a poker table when they'd been dealt an exceptionally good hand. On Clouter's face, the grin turned ugly and Longarm sensed that what he'd hear next would not be pleasant news.

"All I know is that one of them bonds brings in a hundred thousand dollars," he replied. "And a lot of interest money, too, after all this time."

"That's what most people think when they happen to come by one," Clouter said.

"I suppose you're going to say that ain't the way of it." Longarm frowned.

"First of all, let's say you've got a bond that hasn't got Barclay's Bank's name on it," Clouter suggested. "That bond's worth just what you could get for the paper it's printed on. It was put out by the Confederacy, or maybe a bank in one of the Southern states. Chances are if it's one like that, the bank that guaranteed it's not doing business any longer."

"Oh, I've already found out that much."

"I figured you might've." Clouter nodded, then went on, "So let's just say you've got one of the good bonds, one that Barclay's guaranteed. And then let's go on and say you need to cash it in a hurry. I guess you know they only redeem those bonds at their main bank in England. And then Barclay's takes their time making sure it's good. How long do you figure it'd take you to get the cash for it?"

As though the idea was new to him, Longarm frowned for a moment before replying. Then he said, "It'd take a while, I reckon. I ain't sure just how long."

"You'd wait a year, at least," Clouter told him. When Longarm did not reply, he went on, "Now, suppose you bring one of those bonds to me. I'll buy it from you and give you cash, but I'll only pay you a penny or two on the dollar. Not any more than that.''

"But that's only a hundred or two hundred dollars!" Longarm protested.

"Sure."

"And I reckon you'd keep the interest money, too?"

"You're damned right, I would!" Clouter grinned. "I don't do business for my health, Custis. I can wait as long as it takes to get my money back. Chances are, the fellow that's trying to cash in can't."

"It sounds pretty steep to me. I'd need money right bad before I settled for such a little bit."

"Maybe. But most of the ones that come to me with those bonds need cash in a hurry, even if they only get a little bit."

"I can sure see they ain't going to get rich in a hurry if they look to you for help. I ain't so sure I'd want to work for you, either. Not after what you just told me."

"I don't mind spending money on a good man that earns it, Custis," Clouter said. "And you'd be getting more than just your pay. I've got a lot of irons in the fire."

"I sorta figured that from what little you've said. But was I to think about working for you, what is it you'd likely want me to do?"

"Nothing that I don't suppose you haven't done before." Clouter sat silently for a moment, staring at Longarm, then without changing his thoughtful expression he asked suddenly, "Outside of the war, if you were old enough to fight in it, how many men have you killed, Custis?"

"I don't keep score," Longarm replied. "And I don't like to kill nobody unless it's a case of him or me."

"Those weapons you're toting look pretty well used."

"I've used 'em more'n once," he replied, hoping that his curt response would discourage Clouter from pushing the line of their conversation any further.

Clouter's next question ended his hope when he asked, "Would you pull back from drawing it again, if I paid you enough to make it worth your while?"

Longarm sat silently for a moment. He realized only too well that he'd reached a point which he hadn't been able to foresee when the Barclay's Bank sign on the building drew him to look into it. He knew quite well that it would not be easy to turn back unless he abandoned the half-formed plan which had begun to take shape in his mind shortly after meeting Clouter.

"I ain't going to say yes and I ain't going to say no," he replied at last, keeping his voice carefully neutral. "Maybe I could answer you a lot easier if you was to tell me just exactly what it is you got in mind."

"You know anything about wolves? Or coyotes?"

"I've shot a few of both of 'em," Longarm replied. Though Clouter's sudden veering away from the point of their discussion puzzled him, he did not let it show in his voice. "But I don't figure that's what you're aiming at."

"No, it's not," Clouter agreed. "Or on the other hand, maybe it is, if you want to call my gang a pack of wolves. What I'm getting at is that wolves and coyotes run in packs and every pack's got a leader. When the leader starts getting old there's always a young one that sets out to kill him, because that young one wants to be the leader."

"And that's what's happening in your bunch?"

Clouter nodded. "There's a young fellow in my gang that's been acting up. I've seen a few other young bucks do like he's been doing, and I know what it means."

93

"That he's waiting for a time when he can take you in a gunfight that he's certain-sure he'll come out on top of?"

"I figured you'd be smart enough to catch on," Clouter replied. "I don't think he's ready to try facing me down just yet, but the time's not far off when he will."

"And you ain't all that sure you can take him down, so you want somebody else to do the job for you?"

"Somebody like you. Somebody that's good enough with a gun to do it. Whoever I pick out can join up with my outfit, stay as long as they like. Or they can do the job and move on and live like a king for a long time on the money I'm willing to pay them."

"And you're offering me the job," Longarm said. He was not asking a question.

Clouter nodded. "I've got a good gang, Custis, and I aim to stay boss of it as long as I can keep on my feet."

"You look right healthy to me."

"Oh, I'm not hurting yet. But being healthy won't stop a bullet from going into me."

Longarm sat in silence for a moment, then asked, "You made a remark about money a minute ago, but I didn't hear you put out any figures to go with it."

This time it was Clouter who sat for a few seconds without speaking. At last he said, "You've got that bond you want to cash in."

"So I have." Longarm nodded after waiting for Clouter to go on and the other man said nothing more.

Clouter asked at last, "Suppose I said face value for the bond right now. Then after the job's done, I'll give you the interest it's drawn all these years, and a side payment out of my own pocket for half that much more. Would that much hard cash buy your attention?"

94

"It's a pretty good sized chunk of money," Longarm admitted.

"I'd imagine it's a lot more than you generally get for the kind of job I'm talking about. Damn it, Custis! There was a time when I'd've done a job like this one for less than half of what I'm offering you!"

"Go ahead and do it yourself, then," Longarm suggested.

Clouter shook his head. "Not now, not as old as I am. I've got sense enough to know I've slowed down."

"I'll tell you what," Longarm said, standing up. "You give me tonight to think about this deal you're shoving at me. I'll drop by tomorrow and tell you what I've figured out."

For a moment Clouter was silent, then he nodded. "I can't say I grudge you that much time. I'll save you some trouble, too. You'll find the man I'm talking about at the Cottonwood Saloon tonight any time after things start to liven up. His name's Zeph Kilten."

Longarm nodded, then said, "I can find my way out, you don't need to call your man. I'll drop in about this time tomorrow and say yes or no."

Chapter 8

Longarm's expression was very thoughtful as he stepped out of Clouter's office and started along the road leading to the moorings where he'd come from that morning. He reached the line of small sailboats and rowboats tied up at the waterline, bobbing gently at their moorings, and turned off the path. Digging his boot heels into the loose dry earth on the long downslant, he made his way to the line where the dry sand gave way to soggy wetness, only a few paces away from the gentle riplets that ruffled the waters of the bay.

Holding his rifle in the crook of his elbow and dropping his saddlebags on the sparsely grass-clumped sandy soil, Longarm stood for a moment studying the boats that swayed gently in the small wavelets which lapped the shore. Tom's was not among them. Shaking his head, Longarm turned away and started back toward the buildings that stretched widely spaced in a slightly irregular curving line above the waterfront.

"Looks like you'll have to wait a while, old son," he muttered under his breath as he began mounting the gentle slope of shifting sandy soil that rose from the water's edge. "And seeing as how it's been a while since you stretched out on dry land in a real bed that don't rock and wobble and make you miserable half the time, you might as well find a place to light in. This case ain't going to be closed for a while yet, and you're going to need some sleep before you start nosying around again."

Stopping to light a fresh cigar just before he reached the line of buildings, Longarm studied their facades. Though all the houses faced the bay, they had not been built on a common line but were staggered higgledy-piggledy on the crest of the sandy upslope. All of them had two stories, a few rose three. Most of them were built of red bricks, but mixed among the buff-colored brick structures were a few of grey cut-stone and a few more had been framed with wide wooden boards.

There was one thing all of the houses had in common: signs of long misuse or disuse. Here and there along the row boards had been nailed over doors and windows, and in some where boards had not been placed for protection jagged holes showed in panes broken out by weather or vandals of juvenile rock-tossers. With only a few exceptions the boards over the windows were grey and weather-beaten.

On a few of the wooden houses the paint was flaking and peeling away in long strips that rippled like thin banners in the light offshore breeze. On the masonry houses the lines of plaster between the rectangles of cut-stone or the smaller-sized reddish-brown bricks showed black voids here and there where the more friable cement had weathered and fallen away. From some of the chimneys smoke rose in almost transparent threads against the brilliant sun-washed sky.

Longarm resumed his steady walk toward the line of houses, the smoke from his cigar carried in front of him by the off-bay breeze. He stopped when he reached the crest of the slope, and as he looked idly along the line of houses he saw a sign above the peeling paint of the wide veranda of a two-story red brick house almost directly in front of him: ROOMS TO LET. Like most of the other houses along the shore road it had seen better days, but it was only a few steps away.

"It don't seem like you're going to have no trouble finding a place to get some shut-eye, old son," he muttered. "That place don't exactly look like the Brown Palace or even the Windsor, but it's likely to be just as good as the next one you might run into was you to go on to the main part of town. And it sure ain't real likely you'll find another rooming house along here that's as handy."

Shifting his course, he walked to the house and up the steps to the veranda. The door stood ajar. He shouldered through it into a cramped hallway from which a flight of stairs rose. A hand-lettered sign hung from the newel: LANDLADY IN ROOM 3. GO NOCK.

Pushing along the dim hallway, Longarm found the door that bore a square of cardboard with "3" scrawled on it in pencil, and rapped. Faint sounds of movement reached his ears from beyond the door. It opened to frame a grossly fat woman, well past middle age. Her sparse grey hair was pulled into a loose bun atop her head, her face was a series of three blobs: cheeks and chin, and the cheeks pushed high, making her eyes appear as small dark glistening slits.

"Looking for a room, I guess?" she asked.

"That's right, ma'am," Longarm said, nodding.

"Staying long?" the landlady asked without interrupting her inspection of Longarm's rifle and saddlebags. "Or just for the rest of today and tonight?"

"Why, that depends. It might be I'll want to stop quite a while, but I won't know for sure till later on."

"I get fifty cents a day, and I've got two rooms vacant upstairs right now. You won't find any nicer ones anyplace. Both of 'em looks out over the water. If you take one by the week it'd just be three dollars, and that includes a towel and washrag. It'd be ten dollars a month, if you feel like paying in advance for that long."

"Seeing as how I ain't sure yet how long I'll wanta stay, I guess I better pay you by the day," Longarm told her, fishing in his pocket for a half-dollar. He held the coin out to her.

"My name's Valora," she said. "But most folks just call me Val."

"I'm Custis," Longarm replied. "And like I just said, I ain't sure how long I might be here. But I need a place to sleep for a while, and yours was handy."

"Stay as long as you can pay, if you feel like it. But I guess I better tell you, day renters don't get no extras, like towels," she said.

"I expect I can manage without one today."

"I'll expect my rent every day, then, till you make up your mind," Val went on, taking the fifty-cent piece. "You won't have any trouble finding your room, it's Number Six, that's the first one on the right-hand side of the hall if you turn left at the top of the stairs. I don't climb stairs anymore when I don't have to."

"I don't reckon I'll get mixed up." Longarm nodded.

"Bathroom's three doors down the hall. Just be sure to clean up after yourself when you use it."

"I'll remember," he promised.

As Longarm turned away and started toward the stairs he heard the door of the landlady's room click closed behind him. He mounted the stairs and located the room to which she'd directed him. The door was not locked, and there was no key in the inside keyhole when he looked after he'd gone into the room, but a bolt on the inside of the door looked sturdy enough.

More signs of the house's age and decay met his eyes when Longarm surveyed the high-ceilinged chamber. The shade of the big double-sized window had not been drawn and the bright sunshine reflected and amplified from the surface of the bay showed the room in all its beginning decrepitude.

On the door and its frame and on the sills and risers of the broad double window that looked out over the bay what had once been richly smooth varnish was alligatored and flaking away. There were cracks in the plaster of both the walls and ceiling. Some of the cracks had been mended, but the raw white plaster that had been used in the most extensive of the restored areas was already cracking in its center, where a jagged black gap almost wide enough for him to put a finger into broke the surface of the mend. In none of the plastered cracks had the patchwork been painted to match the older dark cream-colored paint that covered the walls.

A threadbare oriental carpet, its colors faded to an almost uniform neutral tan, was spread on the floor's wide boards. The bed's gilded iron frame was worn through in spots, though the bedding looked fresh. The sheet folded back below the pair of thin pillows at the bed's head was glistening white, as were the pillowslips. The bed, a small table beside it, and two straight chairs completed the furnishings. Behind the opened curtains that formed a makeshift closet in the corner there was a line of clotheshooks.

Longarm stood his rifle in the corner nearest the bed, where it would be within easy reach, dropped his saddlebags beside the bed, then shed his coat and vest. He stepped to the window and pulled down the shade, then unbuckled his gun belt and hung it over the head of the bed where he could grasp it without groping.

Levering out of his boots, he stretched luxuriously. His movements brought a squeaking medly of metallic protesting noises from the bedsprings, but the small shifting of his body as he settled down demonstrated that the mattress was less hard and lumpy than he'd feared it might be. He reached for his vest to get a cigar, thought better of it, poked his pillows a few times in search of greater comfort, then settled back and promptly went to sleep.

A whisper of sound, not much louder than the sighing of a sudden hard gust of the offshore breeze whistling through the cracks around the sills of the windows, roused Longarm from his slumber. Sunlight reflected from the bay's water still glowed against the windowshade, and made the room almost daylight bright. The tiny susurrus of sound that had roused Longarm still trickled into the room. He turned his head to the right, then to the left, and a puzzled frown formed on his face when the sound persisted and he was still unable to pinpoint its source.

Spurred by his curiosity, Longarm sat up in bed. He turned his head slowly, straining to listen. He could hear well enough to deduce that the source of the noise must be a conversation between two people. At almost the same moment he discovered that the faint, muted, but continuing sounds were coming into the room from the cracked section of plaster that broke the cream-colored wall at his right side, above the bed.

He was about to pull the blanket up around his ears to shut out the small but persistent noise that had broken his sleep when one of the speakers raised his voice, and for the first time intelligible words reached his ears. The first word he heard drew Longarm's complete attention.

"Custis!" a man's voice said. "I never heard of nobody by that name here in Galveston. Did you?"

When Longarm heard the unknown and invisible man speak the name that he was using in Galveston, he strained still harder to hear what would follow. He did not dare move anymore, for when he'd sat up the bed had responded with the loud squeaking noises of the bedsprings.

"Not as I recall," another man replied.

"You got any idea where the son of a bitch come from, Sid?" the man who'd spoken first went on.

"Damned if I know. All I know is that he's been nosing around. If he finds out about them counterfeit bonds it could be trouble."

By this time Longarm had matched in his memory the voice and the name which had reached his ears. He recognized them as belonging to the man who'd greeted him in such a surly fashion earlier in the day, at the building where he'd talked to Mort Clouter, and belatedly Longarm remembered that Clouter had addressed the speaker as Sid.

Moving as slowly and carefully as he could, Longarm got out of the bed. He made the smallest amount of noise possible as he levered himself to the floor and padded on shoeless feet to the wall. He positioned himself where he could put his ear close to the crack that was allowing the conversation between the two men in the adjoining room to trickle into his own room.

By the time Longarm had settled into the place he'd chosen, the man whose name he did not know was speaking.

"Well," he said, "I've gunned down plenty of men for Clouter before. I've got plenty invested in this phony bond scam. If we had only found the rest of those legitimate bonds we wouldn't of had to plug that other snoop. But I guess that now that I dumped one meddler in the gulf it can't hurt to dump another.''

"That's the only way you can look at it, Sellers," Sid responded. "It's good we got here in plenty of time after Val sent word where he was. Mort wouldn't like it a bit if we'd've missed a chance like this one.''

"I ain't sure I wanta take him when he comes outa his room," Sellers went on. "Val always treated me real nice when she was working the saloons, before she got so fat. I don't like to do nothing that'd give her a bad name now.''

"Val's going to do what Clouter tells her to, just like she always has," Sid replied. "And the best time we can pick for getting this Custis is when he comes out of his room.''

"Oh, sure," Sellers agreed. "We'll be long gone before the law gets here, and there won't be nobody to point a finger at us or Clouter, which is the way he wants things.''

"So all we got to do now is settle down and wait till Custis comes outa his room," Sid went on. "And we better just set quiet and wait till he does.''

Longarm had listened to the conversation between the two waiting gunmen with growing puzzlement. Where were the real bonds? And what had caused Clouter to suspect him? Nothing he'd said to Clouter could have been taken as a threat. On the contrary, Clouter had even offered to help redeem the bonds that were Longarm's passport into the Galveston underworld, then had topped the offer of help with another offer to hire Longarm as his gunmen.

Something's gotta have happened to change Clouter's mind, old son, Longarm now told himself silently. *Question is, what was it, and how'd it come about?*

He pushed the question aside as the two men in the adjoining room resumed their conversation. Longarm had no trouble identifying their voices now. In his new position they reached his ears clearly. He recognized Sellers's voice.

"Damn it," Longarm heard the gunman saying, "I get just a mite edgy when I got to hang around for a long time shut up in a little room like this while I'm waiting to do a job. Chances are that right now Custis is sound asleep in that next room. I got a good notion to bust down his door and get it over with."

"I wouldn't if I was you," Sid said. "You know how mad the boss gets when one of us don't follow orders."

"What's the difference between shooting Custis now and waiting for him to go outside?" Sellers demanded.

"Well, I ain't one to do what the boss told me not to," Sid went on. "But he didn't come right out and say that I wasn't to tell you what he talked about before he made up his mind to send you after this Custis fellow."

"Look here, Sid! It's my neck that'd be stretched if I was to get crossways of the law for killing Custis," Sellers told his companion. "I got a right to know why I'm supposed to handle the job in just a certain way."

"Oh, I sorta feel like you do," Sid agreed.

"Then go ahead and tell me."

"Well, it's—" Sid hesitated for a moment, then went on, "First of all, the boss begun to pick holes in the yarn this fellow Custis had spun about why he'd come here to Galveston. The more he talked, the more holes he pulled in what Custis had told him. That's when he put out the word for anybody who run across Custis to let him know right off."

"Yeah, thinking about how much money he can get for

105

them bonds has had Mort sorta wrapped up for quite a while," Sellers agreed.

"He's still wrapped up in 'em," Sid broke in quickly. "But he begun to get real edgy over the way this fellow Custis popped up outa no place. The more Mort worried about it, the edgier he got. Seems he recalled he'd let drop a few things to Custis that he shouldn't've oughta. That's when he put out the word that he wanted Custis took care of."

"So when Custis rented a room off of Val here, she got the word back to the boss," Sellers said.

"That's about the size of it," Sid agreed. "And that's when he sent me to pass on the job to you."

There was silence in the adjoining room for a moment. Longarm took advantage of the interlude by snaking his boots from the bedside where he'd dropped them and sliding his feet into them. He also took this opportunity to slip into his vest and coat. By the time he'd done that and had his ear pressed to the crack in the wall once more, the pair in the adjoining room had begun talking again.

". . . getting a mite edgy waiting," Sellers was saying. "It don't help my gun hand none when I feel the way I do."

"I don't feel too comfortable myself," Sid admitted.

"I ain't been upstairs here at Val's place for a long time," Sellers went on. "But as I recall, there ain't locks on half the doors."

"That's right," Sid replied. "Just hookeyes."

"A man can kick his way into that next room real easy, then. And that's what I feel like doing."

"It's your job," Sid told the gunman. "All I'm supposed to do is hyper on back and tell the boss you done it."

"And back me up, if I need it," Sellers added.

"Oh, sure. But since I taken that slug in my gun arm when we done that cleanup on the bunch that was trying to push Mort outa Galveston, I don't handle my Colt too good."

"Then you better draw before I bust in the door of that room Custis is in," Sellers told his companion. "Because that's what I'm figuring to do. Give the door one good kick, get my shot off before that Custis dude knows what's going on, and then get the hell outa here."

Longarm recognized the finality in Sellers's words. Planting his feet slowly and carefully on the threadbare carpet he stepped back to the bed and picked up his gun belt. He stepped back and, with the easy familiarity that comes from long habit, strapped the belt on. He felt better with the weight of his Colt on his hip as he pressed his head to the cracked wall again.

". . . split up once we're downstairs," Sellers was saying. Val ain't supposed to come outa her room till she hears us go outside. We'll go out the back door and you go tell Mort I got the job done. I'll head the other way and get lost in town."

"That's the way Mort laid it out," Sid agreed. "And you can get moving now, any time you feel like it."

Longarm waited until the rattle of the doorknob in the room occupied by the two killers reached his ears. Moving silently, he stepped catercornered across the room and pressed his back to the wall beside the door, where it would hide him from the gunman when he opened it.

His wait was not a long one. Though the men coming from the adjoining room moved as silently as they could, he heard the muffled thuds of their feet as they moved along the hall. The distance was short, and they needed

107

only a few seconds to take their places. In the silence that followed their brief advance, Longarm slid his Colt from its holster.

Suddenly the silence was shattered by a loud grating thud as Sellers's booted foot crashed into the door. Longarm could not see the man who came in, but the muzzle flashes of his revolver lighted the room like lightning bolts, and the sound of the two shots that he got off filled the air with noise and powder smoke before the would-be killer realized that the bed was empty.

Now it was Longarm's turn to kick aside the door that had shielded him. As fast as the hired gunman reacted in recovering from his first surprise, he could not bring up the muzzle of his revolver quickly enough.

Longarm triggered his Colt twice, and both slugs went home. Sellers spun around, his frame jerking at the impact of Longarm's lead. His gun barked, but the bullet crashed high into the wall and shattered the plaster around the crack where Longarm had been listening. Then in his dying reflex the gunman got off a second shot, and again plaster showered in chunks from the wall where his first shot had landed.

Longarm did not wait. Certain that his shots had gone home, he stepped quickly around the door and started for the hall. He reached it just in time to see Sid backing away, moving down the hall toward the staircase.

Sid had a revolver in his hand, but he could not raise it to fire before Longarm's lead tore into him. He toppled while he was still trying to raise his revolver, and crumpled onto the stairs where he fell in a huddled lifeless heap.

Longarm heard footsteps thunking in the hallway below. He raced down the narrow hall and reached the head of the stairs. Sid's limp body blocked the staircase. Longarm tried to step over the dead man, but even his long legs could not span the distance to the first open step.

Holstering his Colt, he used both hands to drag away Sid's body, but while Longarm was wrestling with the unpleasant job he heard the slamming of a door from the hallway below and knew that the landlady was getting away from him. The stairway free at last, he took the stairs two at a time, clattering down to the first-floor hallway.

Longarm spun around the newel and hurried to the door of Valora's room. It stood ajar. He yanked it open and stepped inside, but the room was empty.

Chapter 9

Longarm did not waste time searching the cluttered room. He strode swiftly back to the front door and went outside. His eyes searched the curving line of houses, but as far along them as he could see, no one moved.

He circled the house and looked along the graveled street that separated the beachfront houses from those that straggled along it, but none of the small handful of people he saw bore any resemblance to the grossly fat landlady.

"For a woman her size, she sure done a good job of getting outa sight fast," Longarm muttered to himself as he replaced the fired shells in his Colt's cylinder with fresh rounds. "It's dollars to doughnuts she had her a hidey-hole someplace close, all ready to duck into. But from what you heard them two fellows saying, she's as much part of Clouter's gang as they were."

Longarm's mind was racing ahead of his words. Though the day was well along it was far from being over, and he knew that men of Clouter's stripe paid no attention to the clock. Hired killers worked both day and night, and Longarm had no illusions about their tenacity. He realized that when Clouter got word of the failed assassination attempt, he'd be wasting no time in ordering his men to try again.

"It ain't going to take but a little while for Clouter to

send killers back after you, old son," he told himself. "It's a safe bet that them two ain't the only ones he's got. What you need now is a place where you can hole up long enough to figure out your next move, and in a town that you don't know, it ain't going to be all that easy to find one."

Longarm's thoughts reminded him of his gear, which was still in his rented room. He went back into the house and started up the stairs. The lifeless body of the outlaw named Sid half blocked the stairway, but Longarm ignored the contorted corpse and took two steps at a single stride to reach the second-floor hall.

In the room he'd occupied so briefly, the crumpled form of the gunman on the floor looked like a swathed ghost. The body of the man he'd known only as Sellers was almost hidden by the white powdered dust and shards of white plaster that had shattered and fallen from the mended wall during the brief shoot-out. Plaster chunks crunched under Longarm's boot soles as he stepped across the ghost-like shape and went to the corner where his rifle leaned with his saddlebags beside it.

Longarm attended to his rifle before doing anything else. Taking his bandanna from his pocket he first flicked away the heavy coating of plaster dust that had settled on the Winchester, then carefully wiped off the few flakes that still clung to the weapon. His saddlebags were covered almost as totally as his rifle had been. Holding them away from his legs he began removing the dust with more flicks of his bandanna.

He was lifting the saddlebags over one shoulder when he glanced up at the big irregular gaping hole left in the wall where the plaster had fallen away. When the patch fell off, the sturdy timber studding that had been used in framing the house had been exposed. Just above the level of his eyes, resting on one of the horizontal braces that were spaced between the studs, he saw a dust-covered green metal strongbox.

"Well, now," Longarm muttered. "Wonder how long that's been setting up there all hid away. Might be you oughta take a look at it, old son."

Stepping up to the wall, Longarm lifted the box from its resting place. It was surprisingly heavy, and covered with a thick film of dust much darker and finer than that which had fallen on it when the plastered wall shattered. The box was not locked, its lid was secured only by a simple hasp.

Longarm flipped back the lid and his eyes bulged. Gold coins, most of them double-eagles, but with a few Spanish doubloons intermixed, almost filled the box. The remaining space was taken up by a fat envelope. Lifting the envelope, Longarm examined its contents. Though he did not stop to count them, he discovered that he was holding a dozen or more of the $100,000 Confederate war bonds. A quick glance at the first few showed that they bore the guarantee of payment found only on the bonds issued by Barclay's Bank of London. Were these the "real" bonds that the two would-be assassins referred to?

"Old son, you've sure got one hell of a lot of hard cash on your hands now," he muttered under his breath. "More money than you ever expected to see in your life. And sure as shooting these don't belong to the landlady that runs this place, because if they did she wouldn't bother for a minute being the landlady no more. She'd be living in a fine house on snob row in the new part of town."

Longarm picked up the sheaf of bonds and riffled through them, glancing at the signature of the man to whom they'd been issued. As far as his quick inspection revealed, all the bonds had been countersigned by a man named J. C. Nicholson.

"He'd be the man these bonds and the money in this box belong to," Longarm muttered as he carefully replaced the bonds in the box, closed it and secured the hasp. "So whoever he is, old son, you got to find him and give this back. That means you got another job to take care of after you finish your main one."

Dropping to one knee, Longarm opened one of his saddlebags and managed to make room for the strongbox. On his feet again after strapping the bag closed, he hefted the saddlebags and found he could handle the added burden of the gold coins in the box. Sliding the saddlebags over a shoulder, he picked up his rifle and took the long careful step necessary to reach the door.

Ignoring the body that testified to his narrow escape from the hired gunmen, Longarm made his way downstairs. Only a few steps along the hall were needed to confirm his impression that the rooming house was now deserted. He wasted no more time exploring the remainder of the place, but went outside. The sun was sliding down the western sky.

"There's maybe an hour or so of daylight left," Longarm said under his breath as he surveyed the almost deserted shoreline. "And then the kinda animals you're hunting for will be coming out and moving around again. But you got to hole up for that hour, too, or they might be too spooked to come outa their dens."

Only a few small boats were tethered now at the narrow, short wharves that jutted into the greenish-blue water of the bay. In two or three of them men sat bailing out the bilges, in preparation for starting out for a night's fishing. To the west he could see three or four boats on the bay, their sails beginning now to shade from white to rosy pink as the sun itself was changing its hue from golden yellow to a reddish purple as it dropped closer and closer toward the horizon.

For lack of anywhere else to go, Longarm's instinct led him to start toward the shore. His mind was still on the job ahead, and in the habit of men who spend much of their time alone, he continued his conversation with himself as he made his way across the sandy beach.

"Old son, what you got to do is find another hidey-hole real fast and stay outa sight while you pass the time till you're ready to start looking for that Mort Clouter fellow," Longarm muttered as he scanned the shoreline.

When his examination of the surrounding area revealed no place that seemed suitable as a safe sanctuary, he continued on. "Clouter's bound to be the kingpin of just about all the outlaws that's in this place. Seeing as how outlaws don't take kindly to daylight, you got a long time to wait and no place to go to wait in. Trouble is, you still don't know your way around in Galveston, and right now in broad daylight sure ain't no time to start trying to learn about it."

Stopping short of the water's edge, Longarm began walking with the sun at his back, moving parallel to the contour of the shoreline. Across the broad expanse of greenish-blue water he could see the dark line of the mainland, and for a moment he wished that somehow he could reach it and have the luxury of movement impossible on a small island such as Galveston.

Heading away from the old houses and the few small narrow piers that extended in a ragged line to the west, Longarm moved steadily toward the newer and more elaborate commercial wharves that pushed their angular bulk out into the greenish waters of the bay in front of the long row of bulky blocklike warehouses that dominated the next stretch to the east along the shore.

In the bay itself Longarm could see the white sails of a dozen or more small sailboats heading toward the warehouses. The boats themselves were not yet fully visible. They were still indistinct, their hulls not quite above the horizon, and were also half hidden by the hulking bulk and rigging of the big cargo-carrying ships moored at the commercial wharves.

No matter how Longarm squinted and strained his eyes he could not identify the faces of the men on the approaching small craft. The steady off-bay breeze was pushing the little vessels briskly, and the distance closed rapidly as he walked on toward the wharves. Before he'd covered another fifty paces toward the first of the warehouses the distance between him and oncoming flotilla had diminished enough for him to make out details.

Longarm waited until he was only fifty or sixty yards from the first of the long line of warehouses, then he stopped and studied the incoming flotilla.

"Them boats have just about got to be fishing boats coming in," he told himself as he took out one of his long cheroots and lighted it. Through the veil of smoke that whirled around his head, Longarm went on, "And if you're guessing right about it, that means Tom's boat might be one of 'em."

Having no destination in mind, and consequently nothing to lose but a few minutes time spent waiting, Longarm dropped his saddlebags on the sandy shore, leaned his Winchester across them, and stopped to watch as the small flotilla drew closer. As the first few of the boats sailed past, he scanned each one closely without seeing a familiar face.

Finally, near the end of the straggling group and still at a distance that made positive recognition impossible, he saw an arm wave. The boat veered toward the shore, and drew steadily closer until he could see Tom Saunders's familiar face. Topacia was not in the boat with him, and Longarm wondered briefly what had happened, but the small boat was still too far from shore for them to shout back and forth. Then Saunders waved, and when Longarm returned the silent greeting, the young fisherman gestured toward the line of warehouses.

Longarm did not move at once, and Saunders waved once more, then pointed toward the freight wharves for a second time, and this time Longarm got the message. He picked up his gear and started walking toward the big towering buildings and the line of ships at their wharves.

When Saunders saw him moving, he waved again, a sort of salute, and began dropping the taut sail of his little craft. By the time Longarm was within easy speaking distance, Tom had moored the sailboat to a loose line dangling from the stern of the big merchantman in the line of ships that were nestled against the dock.

"Come across the deck of this ship I'm tied to," he called to Longarm. "The water's not deep enough anywhere along here for me to get any closer to shore!"

Longarm looked questioningly at the bulk of the merchantman, its stern towering high above Tom's small craft, but he followed the young fisherman's instructions. A longshoreman's gangplank had been placed to connect the big vessel to the dock and Longarm walked easily up it to the deck. Then he stopped for a moment and gazed at the bewildering maze of rigging that rose between him and the stern.

A few yards at a time, Longarm wound his way through the ropes stretching from deck to masts. He reached the stern rail at last and looked down at Tom in the small fishing boat that swayed in the water below.

"How in tunket do you expect me to get down there?" he called. "I sure ain't going to jump!"

"Of course not!" Tom replied. He raised the coil of rope he was holding. "Catch this coil of rope when I toss it up to you."

Longarm grabbed the flying loosening coil and started to hitch the end of the rope to the ship's rail when Tom interrupted him.

"Not that way!" he called. "Just loop it over the rail and tie your gear to the end, then lower it to me. When I've freed it, I'll snub both ends of the line and you can come down yourself."

Longarm had handled rope very rarely since his early days as a ranch hand, but now his past experience came to his rescue. He followed Tom's directions. First he lowered his saddlebags and rifle, then waited while Tom secured both ends of the looped rope to a cleat on the fishing boat's low rail. Then, letting himself down hand-over-hand, Longarm quickly spanned the distance to the fishing boat.

"You did that just like an old seadog," Tom said as he shook the rope loose and pulled it away from the merchantman. "Somehow I get the idea that you used to be a sailor."

"That's something I never got around to," Longarm replied. "But I did get to be a pretty fair hand with a lasso when I was cowhanding. But what happened to your lady friend? When you and her left, you were figuring on going out together.''

"Topacia? Oh, after we'd talked a few minutes we decided it'd be better not to. She's out there somewhere by herself if she hasn't already put into shore.''

While they talked, Tom was pushing the little fishing boat away from the larger vessel. He trimmed the sail to catch the breeze and the boat began moving slowly forward once more. When he'd put the little craft back on its course he turned once more to Longarm.

"Have you found out anything that's helpful?'' he asked.

"Just that Mort Clouter's sent his gunmen out looking for me,'' Longarm replied. "I had a run-in with 'em already.''

Tom's jaw dropped and he asked, "You mean they tried to kill you?''

"Trying ain't doing,'' Longarm replied. He volunteered no details of his shoot-out with the two gunmen who'd come looking for him in the rooming house.

"And you think they'll try again?''

"Likely they will. But that don't make me no nevermind, except that I want to find Clouter soon as I can and ask him some questions.''

"You don't have any idea why he's got his men after you?'' Tom frowned.

"Not a smidgen,'' he lied. "I figure the only way I can find out is to talk to Clouter himself.''

"Do you know where to find him?''

"Not right now, I don't. But if he don't show up, I'll set out learning.''

"I wish I could give you a clue, Longarm, but I don't have much to do with Clouter and his like.''

"Oh, I don't figure I'll have no trouble. He'll likely be

at that saloon where we was this morning, or another one close by. But from what I've learned on other cases about him and his kind, he won't be showing himself till a lot later on. If the idea don't spook you too much, I guess you better figure on me going with you for a while.''

"You're still the one that's chartering the boat, Longarm. I'm not going to let Clouter's kind bother me.''

"I don't imagine his gun hands are likely to be looking for me on a boat.''

"Probably not. But I don't think it'd be a good idea to tie up at any of the landing places farther up the bay,'' Tom said. He was silent for a moment, frowning thoughtfully, then went on, "If you don't have any objection to staying on the boat a while, we could kill two birds with one stone until it's time to go farther up the island.''

"Doing what?''

"Fishing, of course.''

"When I saw you coming in, I figured you were knocking off for the day,'' Longarm said, puzzled.

"Fish don't pay much attention to the difference between day and night,'' Tom explained. "But this is one of the nights when the cleanup crews from Galveston, the garbage collectors, dump their pickings in the bay.

"That don't make no connection with what I got figured out to do.'' Longarm frowned.

"In just a little while the garbage crews will start hauling all the stuff they've picked up these past couple of days out on scows,'' Tom told him. "They'll go down to the channel between Galveston Island and Pelican Island and dump the garbage. By the time they get to where they'll be dumping, the tide will be making a strong current and it'll carry the garbage out into the gulf.''

"And that's where you aim to fish?''

"It sure is. You see, after they dump two or three loads the sharks start gathering. Most of us fishermen go out on dumping nights and catch a shark or two."

"I never knew sharks were good eating," Longarm said.

"They're not. We just take out their livers and then skin them."

"You mean there's folks that buy shark livers? And shark skins? What in tunket do they want with stuff like that?"

"Doctors buy shark-liver oil by the gallon, when they can get it," Tom explained. "It's not easily come by, and they use a lot of it making medicines. Why, there's three or four doctors' agents here in Galveston just to buy the livers."

"I can see that." Longarm nodded. "But what do they want the skins for?"

"Oh, we sell those to furniture makers. They scrape the skins clean and then dry them and use pieces of them like sandpaper, to put a fine finish on furniture."

"I guess I've heard just about everything now," Longarm said, shaking his head. "But it don't make much nevermind what I do or where I go between now and sometime close to the middle of the night. I figure that's the best time to go looking for Mort Clouter."

"We won't be out but a little while," Tom went on. "The sharks follow the garbage out to sea, so the good fishing only lasts a couple of hours. But if I can catch just one shark tonight, I'll make more money selling the skin and liver than I'd earn fishing for a week."

"Two or three hours won't set me back none," Longarm said. "And like I told you a minute ago, I'm certain

Clouter's got his men out looking for me, so I want to be where they don't have a chance to run across my path."

"I still can't figure why that Clouter is after you."

"That's what don't make sense, Tom. He seemed to take to me when I was talking to him this morning. Unless he was lying to me then, he's changed his mind, and I need to find out why."

"I'd say the best thing we can do until you're ready to look for Clouter is to stay on the water," Tom said thoughtfully.

"That's about the way I look at it," Longarm agreed.

"We'll ride the tide to the channel between the islands," Tom went on. "I'll pitch the anchor over and we can have a bite to eat while we're waiting for the garbage boats to pass us."

"I guess you've got enough grub?"

"Plenty for the two of us."

"Let's do it that way, then." Longarm nodded. "And I'll be right interested in watching you catch a shark outa the water while I'm waiting to go after another shark on dry land."

Chapter 10

"You know, this ain't a lot different from what I've gotten used to in country where there ain't all this water," Longarm remarked.

He shifted his position slightly as the boat heeled a bit, then took a fresh cigar from his pocket and lighted it. The sun had set by now, but the sky still held a slowly fading brightness. The small, widely spaced waves of the oncoming night's breeze were beginning to ripple the water's surface.

Longarm went on, "It didn't cross my mind when you said we'd be riding a breeze that it'd be this much like setting a saddle on a good-gaited horse. You reckon that's why folks who go out in boats call it that?"

"Since I've never been on what you call a good-gaited horse, I've only got about half an idea of what you mean," Tom replied. "But since you mention it that way, I guess you must be right."

"No, sir, this ain't half bad," Longarm went on as he watched the trail of fragrant smoke from his cigar dissipate slowly against the darkening sky. "Now that them stinking garbage boats have passed and the smell's blown away."

"We'll be following them in another few minutes," Tom said. "By this time they'll have finished dumping their loads and be turning around to beat back to their moorings. We won't get much more than a faint smell of the garbage from now on. It's all underwater and settling to the bottom.''

"I guess you're about ready to start rigging up your fishing pole, then?"

"Nobody uses a pole for shark fishing, Longarm. All I'll have is a heavy line and a big hook baited with a chunk of half-rotten meat that I got off one of the garbage scows I passed coming in."

"So that's what I been getting a whiff of now and then ever since I got on the boat with you," Longarm said. "I wasn't about to make any remarks on it, but ever since I got my first whiff of it I've been wondering what it was that made your boat stink so bad."

"You won't be bothered by the smell very much longer," Tom assured him. "I've got my troll all ready to toss over, and there's no reason to wait any longer."

Stepping back to the stern, Tom opened the wood-staved bucket that stood by the tiller. A coil of line the diameter of a man's finger was lying beside the bucket. He lifted it, bringing out of the bucket a big chunk of overripe meat impaled on the biggest fish hook Longarm had ever seen. The hook's shank was almost as large in diameter as the barrel of Longarm's Colt.

With a single practiced swing, Tom tossed the chunk of meat into the water and began paying out the line. It slipped through his half-closed hand for several minutes before going slack, then he pulled the line up until it was taut and looped it loosely over a cleat fixed to the rail.

"Now all we've got to do is wait," he told Longarm. "If we have any luck, we won't have to wait very long.

The garbage that those scows up ahead of us dumped usually brings plenty of sharks into the channel here.''

"I don't guess you'll have no trouble telling when one bites into the bait," Longarm said. "I don't know diddley-squat about sharks, or any other fish for that matter, but I guess they'd give your line a jerk just like a steer gives a lariat when it's lassoed."

"You'll know just as well as I do when one takes the bait," Tom assured him. "They've got a lot more strength than a steer, if you can believe it."

"I can believe a lot about wild critters," Longarm said, nodding. "One time or another, I guess I've tangled with just about any of 'em you could name. Horses and mules and steers, they're a dime a dozen. But I've run up against grizzly bears and buffalo, and one time I don't guess I'll ever forget, there was a loose circus elephant that I got crossways of."

"I don't know that a shark would match an elephant for being strong, but they're about as tough as anything that swims," Tom said. "Whales are stronger, of course, but—"

He stopped abruptly and began swaying in an effort to keep his balance as the boat suddenly jerked, veered, and started to swing around, its stern providing the pivot.

"Shark's taken the bait!" Tom exclaimed. "Now I've got to get it in the boat fast. That hook's going to start its jaws bleeding and the other sharks will be coming after it!"

Before he'd finished speaking, Tom was reaching for the line. Longarm started to rise from the box he'd been sitting on and took a step toward Tom, ready to help if needed. Before he could take a second step the small boat began zigzagging backward through the darkening water.

Longarm stood swaying for a moment, waving his arms

as he fought to keep his balance. Before he could find a safe footing he saw that Tom had already reached the taut line and was tugging on it. The boat's erratic swerving was diminishing and Longarm returned to his improvised seat.

"Yell at me if you need some help," he told Tom. "I ain't used to having anything but solid ground under my feet, but I'll do my best to give you a hand."

"There's nothing much either one of us can do for a minute or two," Tom replied. He'd dropped to his knees at the stern, and was looking at the taut line. "The shark's hooked solid as best I can tell, and until it tires out a little bit we haven't got a chance of bringing it in."

In spite of its taut sails the boat was moving backward now. The line was no longer shaking, but was pulled in a slanting straight line into the water. Tom was working at the rigging now, unwinding the shrouds from the cleats. Suddenly the high triangular sail collapsed and fell to the deck in folds that almost trapped Longarm as they dropped.

He managed to evade the billowing canvas, but now the boat was veering as the shark began towing it in an erratic zigzag. It swam for a short distance in one direction, then changed course unexpectedly to another. The little boat jerked violently with each sudden change the fish made in its underwater efforts to get rid of the hook.

To keep from falling or being thrown into the black water, Longarm dropped to his knees on the sloping boards. If he'd been in a saddle with a bucking, veering horse between his knees, Longarm would have known how to swing his body in responding to the animal's wildest gyrations. In an alien element and facing a strange creature that to him moved unpredictably, for one of the few times in his life Longarm felt almost helpless.

"Just grab something and hang on," Tom called to him.

"The shark can't keep going this way much longer. It'll get tired in a few minutes, and just as soon as it settles down I'll start bringing it in!"

"Well, I ain't to say I'm enjoying this," Longarm told his companion. "But I don't aim to let it buffalo me. I reckon I can hold out all right."

Instead of tiring from its efforts to break free the shark seemed to be gaining fresh strength. For the next few minutes the little fishing boat swung and its mast swayed even more erratically than ever. Then after a particularly prolonged period of jerking around the line suddenly went slack.

"Now's our chance!" Tom exclaimed. "Come give me a hand if you will, Longarm. I'm going to try and bring that damned fish up to the boat."

Longarm managed the few steps necessary to reach Tom, who was hauling in the line hand over hand. After a few false steps Longarm finally got to the stern beside Tom, who was battling the stout line, his knuckles showing white even in the dim night light. Longarm added his considerable strength to the efforts of the young fisherman by grabbing the heavy line and heaving.

Grudgingly, the shark yielded. Its struggles to break free were made at longer intervals and without the furied frenzy that it had shown at first. Longarm and Tom no longer had to loop the slender rope around their hands to maintain control of it, but pulled hand over hand while the heavy line piled up around their feet on the bottom of the boat.

Suddenly the line went slack and the unexpected relaxing of its tension caught Tom by surprise. Involuntarily, he took a leap backward, and as he struggled and staggered trying to keep his balance he crashed into Longarm. Their collision sent both men tumbling into a tangled heap at the

127

bottom of the yawing craft, and as they struggled to regain their feet, their hands still locked around the line, the shark's triangular head shot up over the stern of the little fishing boat.

Both Tom and Longarm froze for an instant when in the dim light they saw the shark's pointed snout and its gaping half-moon-shaped mouth with row after row of glistening white teeth towering above them. Its sharp-pointed nose seemed only an arm's length away. Like a ghost risen from the depths the big fish seemed frozen in place, then slowly it began toppling forward.

Longarm's cramped position slowed his involuntary draw, but only by fractions of a second. His gunhand moved with the speed that had kept him alive in too many shoot-outs to number. He triggered the Colt five times in quick succession. The heavy slugs sped into the shark's gaping jaws with the impact of a dozen sledgehammers.

At least one of the revolver's five leaden bullets tore through teeth and flesh and found a vulnerable spot. It plowed through the shark's pallet and smashed into its brain. For a second or more the huge fish stayed poised high in precarious balance. Half of its tapering body was still in the water, the other half in midair.

Even the smashing impact of the Colt's five rounds could not slow the momentum of the great fish's leap. The shark kept leaning slowly forward, then it dropped across the boat's stern. Longarm and Tom scrambled out of the way just in time as the weight of the big fish landed on the bottom of the boat, shaking and rocking the little craft with its impact.

Despite the five slugs it had taken from Longarm's Colt, the great shark still quivered with life. Its dying tremors were almost as violent as its gyrations had been before its life began to ebb away. Its broad tail was still in the water and lashing furiously. Each time it whipped down to the surface it sent a shower of big drops into the boat.

Longarm got to his feet again and took a half-step toward the shark's tapered snout, which was just beyond his reach. Tom grabbed him quickly and pulled him back.

"Don't get too close!" he said. "Sharks take a good while dying. This fellow's still dangerous. It could take off an arm or a leg if you happened to brush against it."

"That's sure one hell of a big fish!" Longarm gasped. His eyes were riveted on the spasmodic quivers that still shook the creature now and then. "How in hell do you know when it's finally dead?"

"You don't. I've seen sharks that hadn't moved for five minutes or so, sharks I'd thought were dead, come back to life and clamp their jaws on a man that touched them. We'll just have to stay clear of it for a little while longer."

"Maybe I better reload and get a few more bullets into it," Longarm suggested.

Tom shook his head. "It wouldn't do much good. That lucky shot you put into its brain killed it, but the shark doesn't know it yet. Give it a few minutes more. You can tell when it's safe to go close to it. While we're waiting I'll light a lantern so we can see what we're doing."

Longarm stood silently, watching the shark while Tom got a ship's lantern from the boat's small stowage and lighted it. In the glow the shark looked even more formidable than ever. After what seemed to Longarm an interminable time the big fish quivered violently and its tail splashed on the surface of the water, sending up another showering spray. Then it lay still.

"It's dead now," Tom told Longarm. "And I'm going to skin it right where it is. Then I'll take out the liver, and when that's done we'll push it into the water."

"I'll help you all I can," Longarm offered. "I don't reckon there's all that much difference between a shark and a steer, and I've gutted and skinned enough steers to know a little bit of what I'm about."

"I'll be glad for some help." Tom nodded. "It won't take long because the skin peels pretty easy once it's started.

With the skilled precision of a surgeon, Tom girdled the huge fish where its body began to bulge above the tail. He pulled a flap of its skin forward, and showed Longarm how to roll it ahead of his quick, sure knife strokes. When the cuts reached the fish's head, he detached the skin from the carcass and laid it aside. Three swift deep slashes bared the liver, which Tom tossed into a bucket.

"I'll pull up the anchor and set the sails now," he told Longarm. "And we'll be on our way back."

"What about the shark?"

"We'll push it over the stern soon as we start moving. Any chunk of meat this big draws every shark that's close by, and this water's going to be all churned sooner than you'd believe."

"Well, I won't say I ain't glad to be moving again," Longarm said. "Because we been out here quite a while, and I'm hungry enough to take a bite of that damn shark."

"Don't," Tom advised. "Some people eat shark meat, but I don't like the taste of it myself."

"I didn't say I was about to cut me off a slice of shark." Longarm grinned. "I can wait till we get to shore. And then after we've had supper it'll be time for me to go out and get started looking for Mort Clouter."

"From what little I've heard about him, he can be a hard man to find when he wants to be," Tom said. "But maybe I can help you find him."

"That ain't part of the job I hired you for. But if you've got an idea I can use, go ahead and spit it out."

"It's common gossip along the waterfront that if somebody wants to find Clouter, all they have to do is step into the first saloon they pass and leave word they're looking for him. If he's interested enough in what they want to see him about, Clouter will find them right away."

Longarm had encountered the same grapevine in other towns where a single powerful criminal held the unofficial title of underworld boss. He nodded and said, "That's sorta what I was wondering about."

"It's the only help I can give you," Tom said. "Aside from teaching you how not to catch sharks."

"One lesson in shark fishing's enough," Longarm replied. His voice took on a sterner tone as he went on, "When I set out on a case, I aim to close it up. Right now all I can do is what the little boy done to the doughnut, just keep nibbling away till there ain't nothing left but the hole. There's lots of money tied into this case and money always means trouble."

"Speaking of money, I've got to finish a job myself before too much longer. I'll have to get that shark's liver to old Doc Tolliver while it's fresh. In another hour or so it'll start getting rancid and he won't buy it from me."

"I don't have to be so persnickety about moving around, now that it's nighttime," Longarm said. "Supposing you just run up to shore wherever you've got to go, and after I've given the town a little bit of a look-see, I'll mosey on shank's mare down to where we was last night."

"It's a pretty long walk down to the old part of town."

"I need to stretch my legs after cramping 'em up for such a long time in this little boat."

"Suit yourself, then." Tom nodded. "I'll put in as soon

as we get to the wharf at the end of Sixteenth Street. That's in the new part of town. Doc Tolliver's office is on Church Street, and that's not too far from the waterfront.''

"That's all just gibberish to me,'' Longarm told his companion. "But I'm used to finding my way around in new places. I'll make out all right. It won't take me long to get a bite to eat and then find my way out to where I got a chance to run into Clouter.''

"What about tomorrow?''

"I don't figure to take no more boat rides till it's time for me to report back to the marshal's office in Houston, Tom. That won't likely be for another day or so.''

"Then just leave word for me at Donovan's Saloon. I'll be fishing days, but I'll drop in every time I put in and see if you need the boat again.''

"I've been thinking, Tom,'' Longarm went on. "It's time I got me a room in a hotel. I sure ain't going to try sleeping in another strange boardinghosue unless it's in a pinch. Besides, I can leave word for you whenever I need your boat again.''

"Try the Washington Hotel,'' Tom suggested. "It's not the newest or fanciest place in Galveston, but it's right downtown and handy to the landings. I'll stop in there now and then as well as Donovan's to see if you've left me a message.''

Tom had swung the rudder to angle the boat toward shore as they talked. Galveston's lights were already separating into individual pinpoints instead of a blurred glare of brightness.

While they were covering the last gap to the wharf, Longarm busied himself with his preparations. He reloaded his Colt and put a handful of fresh ammunition into his capacious coat pocket, then placed his saddlebags and rifle where they would be in easy reach when the boat was tied up.

He waited until Tom finished tying up to the pier between two towering masted merchant ships and climbed the short ladder up to the dock, then handed up his own gear and the pail that held the shark's liver before climbing up to the wharf himself.

"I guess we'll see each other tomorrow or the next day," Tom said. "If you go down two streets and turn left you'll see the Washington Hotel about halfway down the street."

"I'll find it without no trouble," Longarm said. "And you be sure to leave word there in case you hear anything that might be helpful."

They parted then. Longarm started up the dark street that Tom had indicated. There were only a few pedestrians, all of them seeming to be in a hurry. Lights glowing at the top and bottom of a pair of swinging doors on the street ahead reminded him of Tom's suggestion. Longarm pushed through into the saloon.

There were only three other customers in the place. They were clustered together with the aproned barkeep at one end of the long bar, but his eyes were following Longarm as he stepped across the sawdust-covered floor and stopped near the center of the bar. The barkeep left his low-voiced conversation to come and serve him.

"Tom Moore, if you've got any," Longarm told the man. As he spoke he dropped a silver cartwheel on the bar.

"Sorry, friend, but that's one we can't afford to handle," the man replied. "If it's rye whiskey you fancy, though, I can oblige you without any trouble."

Longarm nodded and the man took a bottle from the

array along the backbar. Placing it and a shot glass in front of Longarm, he made no move to pick up the money. Longarm took a cigar from his pocket, clamped it between his teeth and lighted it. As he'd anticipated, the barkeep started up a conversation while Longarm was puffing the cigar into life.

"From the gear you're packing, I'd say you're a stranger in town," the man suggested. "But I don't recall that there's any passenger ships putting in at this time of the night."

"I didn't come over on one," Longarm replied. He did not volunteer any further information, but gave his full attention to filling the glass in front of him.

"Business, I suppose?" the barkeep asked.

"Mostly. But I don't rightly know where I'll have to go to find a man I'm looking for."

"He'd have a name, I guess? Maybe I can help."

"His name's Clouter," Longarm answered, keeping his eyes on the barkeep's face as he sipped the pungent whiskey. He tipped the glass to his lips and drained it. Though the barman's professional smile did not change, Longarm saw his lips and eyelids twitch. As he put the glass down on the bar he picked up their interrupted conversation. "Mort Clouter," he repeated. "You happen to know him?"

"I've heard the name," the barkeep replied noncommittally. "But Galveston's grown into a pretty good sized place now, and I'm not what you'd call acquainted with him."

"No more am I," Longarm replied. "That's why I want to get hold of him."

"I imagine he'd have to know your name if he wants to see you."

"I imagine he would. It's Custis."

"And it's easy to see you're a stranger here," the barkeep repeated. "I tell you what, Custis, I always like to help folks that've just got to Galveston. I'll do some asking around, and if you don't find him tonight, stop in tomorrow."

"That's real friendly of you," Longarm said. I'll do just that." He refilled his glass and emptied it with two large swallows, and when he'd put it back on the bar, gestured to the coin which still lay untouched. "Buy yourself a drink outa what's left of that. I been going for a long time today, and I can use some shut-eye."

Before the barkeep could reply, Longarm had picked up his saddlebags and turned to go. He stepped into the salty night air trailing a veil of smoke from his cigar, and started toward the hotel Tom had suggested.

"Well, you done two kinds of fishing tonight, old son," he told himself quietly. "One shark landed and the bait tossed out to bring in a bigger one. Now you can go to bed and catch up on your shut-eye and wait for that bait to do its work."

Chapter 11

When Longarm awoke in the subdued light of the strange room he knew at once where he was and that he was very hungry. He glanced at the thin faint lines of light that crept around the edges of the drawn shades and filtered into the room through the heavily embroidered net curtains of the room's tall windows.

At first glance he was sure that the dimness of the glowing vertical strips indicated pre-dawn. He looked for a second time while he lighted his wake-up cigar and frowned as he realized that the quality and brightness of the light was not that of dawn. Rolling off the bed he walked on bare feet to the nearest window and pulled the shade aside.

A burst of sunshine reflected in a brilliant silvery glare off the windows of the building across the street from the hotel. When the reflected light hit his eyes they started watering. Longarm blinked the moisture away. He gazed at the glowing circular reflection of the morning sun that appeared on each of the windowpanes, then dropped the shade quickly and started back across the room toward the bed.

"It ain't no wonder that your belly thinks your throat's been cut, old son," he muttered as he got back to the bed and sat down, reaching for his clothing on the chair beside the bed. "You ain't got outa bed this late since Hector was a pup."

After stamping into his boots while he strapped on his pistol belt, Longarm dug into his saddlebags and brought out his wrinkled frock coat. The green metal strongbox he'd found at the rooming house had been on top of the coat, and Longarm looked at it thoughtfully while he was shrugging into his coat.

His stomach was sending out distress signals now. Deferring any other business, Longarm did not open the box, and wasted no time in finding the stairway to the hotel lobby. It was deserted except for the desk clerk. He walked across to the dapper young man, who looked up from the ledger in front of him and raised his eyebrows enquiringly.

"I reckon there's a café someplace close?" Longarm asked. "And a barbershop? I don't recall noticing much of anything last night when I was coming here."

"You'll find both on the premises, sir," the clerk told him. Pointing to a corridor that led off the lobby he went on, "Just down the hall, there. And if I might suggest, sir, we also have a tailor available who will be glad to press your coat for you, if you wish."

"I'll leave it with him after breakfast"—Longarm nodded—"and I got some other clothes he can tend to at the same time."

An hour later, his stomach no longer rebelling and his cheeks still tingling with bay rum from his shave, Longarm returned to his room. Doffing his freshly pressed coat and his hat, he followed his morning habit and went over his rifle and Colt inch by inch, checking their loads and rubbing their blued steel surfaces with the scrap of soft oil-saturated wool that traveled with him in his saddlebags.

He gave the same careful attention to the stubby little

derringer that was linked to the end of his watch chain. Then he sat down on the bed and opened the strongbox. This time there was no need for him to hurry. He took out the packet of Confederate States bonds and inspected each of them carefully.

As he'd suspected after the first hasty look he'd given them at the rooming house, all the bonds had been issued and guaranteed by Barclay's Bank. Each of them had also been countersigned by the same man: J. C. Nicholson. Longarm paid no attention to the money in the box other than to rearrange the coins so the bonds could be fitted into the metal container more easily.

"Old son," he said thoughtfully, "there's got to be some kind of connection between this box and that place where you found it and that fellow Clouter. Him being the kingpin outlaw here, if there's crooked work going on, he'd be in it up to his belly button, sure as God made little green apples."

Slipping a cigar out of his vest pocket, Longarm flicked his thumbnail across a match and lighted up. Leaning against the crumpled pillows while swirls of fragrant smoke coiled around his head, he let his thoughts ramble on.

"What you got to do now is find out what sorta tie-in there is between Clouter and this fellow Nicholson. All you got to work from is them two names, and you already know about Clouter. Maybe Nicholson is the lead you been looking for to get to the bottom of this business that's got the Treasury Department all roiled up. So the thing to do is figure out how to go about digging up that missing link."

Even as his first thought flashed through Longarm's mind it was being pushed away by another. "Now, a man here in Galveston that could leave all this loose money and close to a million dollars worth of bonds ain't just no johnny-come-lately. There's bound to be folks that'll know where you can find him, and lollygagging around ain't going to get you no place."

Now that his thoughts were in order, Longarm wasted no more time. He donned his coat, put on his hat, tucked the green steel box under his arm and returned to the lobby.

"Maybe you can help me a little bit," he said to the desk clerk. "There's a man here in Galveston that I need to find. His name's Nicholson, J. C. Nicholson. You ever heard of him?"

"Why, everyone in Galveston is familiar with the name Nicholson," the clerk replied. "He's one of the most respected, and I might also say one of the wealthiest, of our citizens. Any cabman you hail will be able to take you to his home. It's near the new Beach Hotel, on Tremont Street, I believe."

"I ain't all that well acquainted with Galveston yet," Longarm said. "But from what you said, I judge it'd be a mighty far piece to walk."

"Very far. It's on the south side of the island. Unless you're fond of walking and have a great deal of time, I would certainly suggest a carriage. I'm sure you'll find one or two waiting outside the hotel."

"That's all I need to know." Longarm nodded. "Thanks for the information."

There were indeed three carriages waiting at the curb outside. Longarm stopped at the first one in line and asked, "How much of a fare do you want to take me out on Tremont Street?"

"You'd want to come back, too, I suppose?" the plug-hatted cabbie asked.

"I suppose. But my business out there ain't going to take but a few minutes to wind up."

"Then if I don't have to set waiting too long, missing the fares I'd pick up here, I'll make you a good price. A dollar each way. If I got to wait long for the trip back, call it a dollar going, dollar and a half coming back."

"Why, in Denver—" Longarm began, then he stopped abruptly and nodded. "All right. We got a deal. And I ain't sure how long it's going to take me to get my business done out there, but I'll try not to keep you waiting."

Until now, Longarm's activities on Galveston Island had kept him confined to the waterfront. Now he got his first good look at the town that bore the island's name as the hackman wheeled his carriage out onto Twenty-second Street and followed it to Tremont, where he turned and headed south. From what Longarm saw, his impression was that the town was having a builders' picnic, for in almost every block one or two new buildings were going up.

At the beginning of his ride, business buildings predominated the construction, with sprawling stores and tall tiers of offices. The style of building changed when the carriage jarred off the noisy brick pavement after crossing Broadway and rolled more smoothly and quietly over the crushed oyster shells that now paved the street. Now the big chalk-white blocks of cut-stone favored for stores and office buildings were seen less often, and red bricks and wide white-painted boards took their place. The buildings were no longer pushed together cheek by jowl, and green lawns stretched between them.

While some of the houses were small, one-story bunga-lows, a number of them had two stories and a few rose to

141

three. Most of the small bungalows looked alike, as though they'd been built according to a single plan. The larger structures revealed more elaborate design and the details they featured often verged on the whimsical. Few had windows of uniform size, but ranged from big bays and elaborate expanses of stained glass to small, high-set peek-aboos. Almost without exception the lawns that surrounded them were carefully manicured, broken by trees and shrubs and often small flower beds.

Gradually the houses grew less numerous, more widely spaced and more elaborate. Most of them towered to three stories, and turrets and minarets and circular corners that were topped with conical roofs gave them the mark of individuality. Their lawns were wider, with more and bigger flower beds breaking their green expanses. Some were cut by circular drives paved with crushed oyster shells that curved past columned porticos and elaborate entryways.

Longarm realized that now he'd passed into the domain of Galveston's very rich families. He was not surprised when the hackman reined into a graveled driveway that led to one of the largest of the houses and pulled up under a porte cochere. Longarm was out of the hack almost before it stopped. He started toward the door, but before he reached it the door swung open and a black man in sober unadorned green livery stepped out.

"I am sorry that I was not quicker to greet you, sir," the black man said. "But there are no guests listed in madam's book to call today."

"I didn't come calling on the lady of the house," Longarm replied. "It's Mr. J. C. Nicholson I'm looking for. Ain't this the right place?"

"Yes, sir, it is the Nicholson residence. But the master

is not in. He's in Austin, at the request of Governor Ireland. May I—'' he broke off, interrupted by a woman's voice calling from the doorway.

''Who's come to call, Joseph?'' she asked.

Turning to reply, the servant said, ''A gentleman looking for the master, Miz Phoebe.''

''Oh,'' she said. ''I thought perhaps—well, I'm sure you can explain to the gentleman.''

By this time Longarm was looking toward the doorway. He saw a woman framed in the open door. She was close enough for him to see her clearly. She looked to be in her middle thirties, perhaps even a bit younger, for he saw no signs of wrinkles on her smooth creamy face and her pouting lips were full and red. She wore her auburn hair draped high to expose her ears and gathered into a loose bun at the nape of her neck. Even in the billowing white dress she had on Longarm could see the bulges of her generous breasts and the swell of her hips.

Speaking over the shoulder of the liveried servant, Longarm asked, ''I reckon you'd be Miz Nicholson?''

''Yes, I am. But—''

''Excuse me for interrupting, ma'am,'' Longarm broke in, ''but I'm a United States deputy marshal here in Galveston on a case, and I need to talk to somebody in your family right away. Can you spare me a few minutes of your time?''

''Why, I suppose so, if it's important.'' She turned to the servant and went on, ''Show the gentleman to my sitting room, Joseph. And bring us—'' She raised her head to look at Longarm and asked, ''Would you enjoy a julep, Mr.—''

''Long, ma'am. Custis Long,'' Longarm replied to her unasked query.

143

"Mr. Long," she asked, "can I offer you something else than a julep? Something you'd like better?"

"Well, ma'am, I don't hold much to fancy mixed-up drinks. If it ain't too much trouble, I'd as lief just sip a tot of plain old straight whiskey. Rye, if I ain't being too forward."

"Of course you aren't," she said, smiling. Over her shoulder she said to the servant, "See to it, Joseph, and don't forget that I'd like a julep myself. I'll show Mr. Long the way to my sitting room." Turning back to Longarm, she went on, "Just come along with me, Mr. Long. I get the impression that your business here is urgent, and that box you're carrying must have some part in it. I won't ask questions about it now, and I'll be glad to help if I can."

Tucking the green box under his arm, Longarm followed her to the entry door, which the servant was holding open. She led him through one elaborately furnished room and then another, into a small sitting room. It was more informally decorated, with a suite of white wicker furniture upholstered in brightly hued patterned fabric. She indicated the divan with a gesture to Longarm and settled into a wide rocking chair.

"Now, Marshal Long"—she smiled—"suppose you tell me what's brought you here? Since my husband died, this has been a very quiet place. Young James doesn't always take me into his confidence the way his father did."

For a moment Longarm stared at her. He kept his face from showing his surprise as he asked, "You mean that you ain't—I mean, your husband ain't—"

"My husband was James C. Nicholson senior," she replied. "He passed away several years ago. My stepson is

James junior. He's been handling all the family's affairs since his father's death.''

"Well, now," Longarm said, trying to reorganize his thoughts and not quite sure of what he should say next. "I'd say I better start out by asking you a question or two.''

"Go ahead," she invited. "My late husband took me into his confidence quite completely. If the matter that brought you here concerns him, I'm sure I can be helpful. If it's something that has to do with James junior, you'll have to wait until he finishes whatever business Governor Ireland called him to Austin to handle and returns from there.''

Longarm had regained his poise by now. He said, "No, I reckon you're the one that I need to talk to, even if I didn't know anything about what you just told me.''

"Since you understand our family relationships now, I can guess that whatever brought you here concerns my late husband," she said. Before she could continue, Joseph came in carrying a tray holding glasses, a bottle, and a pitcher. She motioned toward a small table close at hand and told him, "I'll attend to the serving, Joseph. You may go now, and please see that we're not disturbed.''

After the manservant had left Longarm said, "What I guess I better do is ask you a question or two.''

"I'll be glad to answer them," she assured him. She stood up and stepped over to the table as she went on, "But let me fill our glasses first.''

She filled a small glass from the whiskey bottle and a large one from the pitcher and brought Longarm his drink. At close range for the first time he could see a few scattered strands of grey in her auburn hair and the fine lines of aging on her face. She took her glass with her to the chair she'd been occupying and settled back in it.

"Ask your questions, Marshal. I'll do my best to answer."

"Well, now," Longarm began. He took a healthy sip of the whiskey before going on, "I suppose you've been wondering about what brought me here. First off, there's a big old house out along the waterfront west of town. Did it by any chance belong to your late husband?"

"Of course. The old Nicholson homestead. My husband—" She stopped, shook her head and went on, "I was my husband's second wife, Marshal Long. His first wife died giving birth to James junior. My late husband and I were married three years later. He'd already started to build this house before the first Mrs. Nicholson passed away. But why did you come all the way out here to ask about the old house? Anyone in Galveston could've told you it belonged to my late husband's family."

"You're being real open and aboveboard with me, ma'am," Longarm replied. "And I'll be the same way with you. I found this box I got here all plastered up in a wall inside of that old house I was asking you about. It's full of money, and there's a bunch of old Confederate bonds in it, too. The bonds—"

"Are made out to my late husband?" she broke in. Longarm nodded and she went on, "And you've come to return them?"

"Oh, sure. I don't reckon your family's got much need for the money, but the box is yours by right. Except I'm going to ask a favor of you where these bonds are concerned."

"What sort of favor?"

"I figure to use 'em for bait," Longarm explained.

146

"Bait?" She frowned.

"Yes, ma'am. You see, these old bonds can still be cashed in for good American money, and there's a gang at work down here trying to get all of 'em they can get their hands on, by hook or crook. The U.S. Treasury is real concerned about it."

"You don't have to give me all the details of your case, Marshal Long," she broke in. "My late husband saw to it that I learned about the inner workings of high finance."

"I can't say that I've picked up all the curves and curlicues of the case myself yet," Longarm admitted. "Because the high-muckety-mucks back in Washington are trying to keep things just as quiet as they can right now, and I'll have to ask you to do the same."

"Of course," she agreed readily. "You understand that I'll have to tell my stepson. You can depend on him to keep very quiet, too. But he's not likely to be back soon, so you'll quite likely have your job finished when he does return."

"Well, now, I might and I might not," Longarm told her. "But I got a sorta scheme that I'm working on. And if it comes out all right, I'll get my case closed pretty fast."

"That's exciting," she said. "Is it a secret, or could you give me a hint about it?"

"Matter of fact, I been trying to figure a way how I could get around to asking if you'd give me a little bit of help."

"I don't see how I could help you," she said.

"Maybe a society lady like you never has heard about the man that seems like the kingpin crook here in Galveston. But I—"

"You're talking about Mort Clouter?" she broke in.

"That's him all right."

147

"Everyone in Galveston knows his name and reputation. How is he involved in your case?"

"It'd take a long time to go into all the ins and outs of that," Longarm replied. "But I got a scheme halfway figured out that might help me put him behind bars and save a lot of good folks a whole passel of money and trouble."

"That sounds interesting, but I don't suppose you'd feel free to talk about it."

"I'd rather not right now, ma'am. But Clouter's smart and crooked both. All I can tell you now is that you'd be doing me a right big favor if you'd lend me the use of them bonds for a few days so I can bait my trap with 'em."

"Now that sounds even more interesting than ever."

"You'd sure be doing me a real favor, ma'am."

For a moment Phoebe Nicholson was silent, then she said thoughtfully, "I suppose I have as much say about those bonds as my stepson does. And I don't think that he'd object to having them used to trap a criminal."

When she fell silent Longarm waited for a long moment before asking, "You think you can see your way to letting me use 'em to trap Clouter with?"

"Clouter's a scab on Galveston's good name," she went on. "Of course you can use the bonds, Marshal Long, if they'll help you put him in jail."

"Well, I'm right obliged to you," Longarm told her. "I just wish I could tell you how much."

For a moment she did not reply. Then she smiled and nodded and said, "I think perhaps you can."

"I guess I don't follow you." Longarm frowned. "Now, I can see how you'd help me out of the sorta bind I'm in, but—"

She broke in. "I've been in what you call a sort of bind myself, Marshal Long. And I've a feeling that you're the kind of man who could help me break out of it."

"I don't see how," Longarm replied. "You ain't the sorta lady that goes around getting into trouble. All I got to do is look at you to tell that. If you feel like explaining—"

"I'd rather show you than tell you," she replied, standing up. "Come along with me and you'll have your explanation."

Without waiting for Longarm to stand up, Phoebe Nicholson turned and started toward the door at the back of the room. Trying to keep his confusion from showing on his face, Longarm got to his feet and followed her.

Chapter 12

A flight of stairs rose at the end of a short corridor, and still without looking back Phoebe started up the carpeted steps. Longarm was close behind her. As he mounted the stairs he caught a whiff of the subtle trail of perfume left by the woman ahead of him. She led him along a wide corridor, broken by several doors, until she stopped in front of one and for the first time glanced back as though to make sure that Longarm was still there. Then she opened the door and went through it.

When Longarm stepped into the room she had turned and was facing him. She was smiling, but the quick flickering movements of her eyes told him that she was nervous. He glanced quickly around the room. It was furnished with the simplicity of luxury: a wide high-backed mahogany double bed with a nightstand beside it, a matching wardrobe and a dressing table fitted with a ceiling-high mirror, and two or three chairs.

"You seem to be an understanding man, Marshal Long," Phoebe said. "So I'm sure you can figure out why I've brought you up here. Since I did, and we're together in private, I'm going to ask you to be understanding and help me. But I'll tell you in advance that I've made up my mind, and I hope you won't ask me to change it."

Longarm was beginning to feel more at ease. This was not the first time a woman had invited him to her bedroom after a brief acquaintanceship.

"I reckon I got a right fair idea of what you invited me up here for," he replied. "And you're a right pretty lady. But it sorta seemed like—"

"Let me tell you my side first," Phoebe broke in. "My late husband and I had only been married for a bit over a year when he began to ail. Another year passed before he died. For the past two years I've been in mourning, out of respect for the family's good name. But I'm still young, Marshal Long!"

Longarm began to feel firmer ground under his feet now. He also felt a surge of sympathy for her. He said, "I got to agree with you, ma'am. And real pretty, too."

A smile flashed over her face, then her expression changed to a look of dismay. "Do you know what it's like to be in mourning, Marshal? A year inside this house, only going out once a week, to church on Sundays? Wearing nothing but black dresses for two years? And only going out to funerals and such for the second year? And no man talking to you like a woman needs to be talked to, let alone taking you in his arms and loving you like a woman needs to be loved?"

"Well, I can see it'd be somewhat of a—" Longarm began.

She cut him short. "During this past year I made up my mind that I was going to grab the first good-looking man I met and take him to bed. And you're that man, Marshal! Can you say truthfully that you blame me?"

"I can't say as I do," Longarm admitted. He was feeling something besides sympathy now. Phoebe looked even prettier than before, with her eyes flashing and her full red lips pouting indignantly. Now that his first surprise had dissipated, the invitation that she offered was beginning to interest him.

"Then did I bring you up here just to disappoint me? Or are you the kind of man I've taken you to be?"

"Well, I never was one to say no to a pretty lady," he confessed. Without taking his eyes off Phoebe he began to shrug out of his coat.

Phoebe needed no further encouragement. She stepped up to him and lifted her face invitingly. Longarm proved the truth of his last words by bending to kiss her. They'd held the kiss for only a moment before her tongue darted out and parted his lips. Longarm met the offered caress with his own tongue while he pulled Phoebe to him. She wrapped her arms around him and clamped him in an eager embrace as their tongues entwined and prolonged the kiss until both were breathless. Longarm did not want to break away first, and he waited until Phoebe drew back her head to look up at him.

"I want a lot more than a kiss, Marshal Long," she said.

Her eyes were open wide and Longarm saw eagerness in them as well as in her full quivering lips. He said, "I aim to give you a lot more. But if we're going to bed together—"

"We are!" she exclaimed. "As soon as we undress!"

"Then I guess we better do something about undressing," he suggested. "And maybe before we get any further along, I oughta tell you that I got a nickname I answer to faster'n I do what you been calling me. It's Longarm."

"Longarm!" she repeated. "That's what you'll be to me from now on."

As she spoke Phoebe was sliding her hand down his side. She pushed it between their close-pressed bodies and began caressing his burgeoning erection. Longarm was busy shedding his coat. He let it fall to the floor and managed to work his hand between them to unbuckle his gun belt. He lowered it to the floor on top of his coat.

Phoebe did not remove the hand that was caressing him through the fabric of his trousers. Her eyes were half closed as she fondled him. Longarm began fumbling with the line of small, closely spaced buttons at the back of her dress. She made no effort to help him, for both her hands were busy now. Without releasing her grip on his crotch she'd brought her free hand around and was unbuckling his belt.

Longarm's big fingers had finally found the combination to the small buttons of her dress and he was unfastening them as quickly as he could. He bent forward and started trailing kisses over Phoebe's neck and shoulders while she continued her attentions to the buttons of his fly. She began unbuttoning them, and when she'd gotten the first two or three loose she pushed his trousers down his hips.

By this time Longarm had unbuttoned most of the tiny buttons of Phoebe's dress. He pulled the dress over her shoulders, and when she felt his fingers brushing her bare skin Phoebe stopped pushing his tight-fitting trousers down his hips.

"We're acting like a couple on their honeymoon," she said. "Let's just take our clothes off as fast as we can and go to bed where we'll be comfortable."

"Now, that suits me to a tee," Longarm agreed.

They stepped apart and Longarm levered out of his boots, then finished removing his trousers. He dropped them on top of his coat and added his vest and shirt to the heap while Phoebe was stepping out of her dress and chemise. Longarm was pushing his long johns down his thighs when Phoebe looked up and saw his jutting erection.

154

"Oh, my!" she exclaimed. "Hurry, Longarm! I can't—"
She was stepping to his side as she spoke and Longarm
kicked his feet free of his underwear just in time to catch
her as she left her remark unfinished and lurched forward
to throw her arms around him and lever herself upward,
seeking another kiss.

Longarm sensed her intention and braced himself as she
spread her thighs and released one arm from her embrace
to grasp his rigid shaft and position it. She wrapped her
legs around his hips and pulled herself to him. As he sank
into her she sought Longarm's lips again and he bent his
head to meet them.

Phoebe tightened her legs in a quick clasp that pulled
Longarm into her more deeply. Longarm was so ready to
move now, he was almost as eager as she was. He took
two long steps that carried them to the bed and fell on top
of her as he bent to lower her to the high mattress.

"Now drive!" Phoebe whispered in his ear. "And don't
stop even if I ask you to! You just don't know how good it
feels to have you inside me!"

Longarm started stroking and Phoebe cried out with joy
as he began his slow rhythmic movement. He'd been
driving into her for only a few moments when she began
trembling and loosing small breathy cries that started in
her throat.

"Faster now!" she urged. Her voice was low and broken by her gasps. "I can't wait! But don't stop! This is
what I've been dreaming about and I don't want to wake
up!"

Longarm had no thoughts of stopping. Phoebe's moans
soon became a string of small screams that died, smoth-
ered in her throat. Her body was writhing under Longarm
now and he felt her heels digging into his back as she
pulled her hips upward to meet his steady thrusts.

"Deeper, Longarm! Go deeper!" she urged between her quickening gasps. "I've waited a long time for a man like you!"

Phoebe's hips were jerking upward spasmodically now and her neck was arched backward. Longarm bent his head to caress her throbbing throat with his lips and tongue and her hands dug into his back.

"I can't wait for you, Longarm!" she gasped. "But don't stop!"

"Don't worry, I ain't about to," he promised.

Phoebe was writhing frantically by now. A moaning cry began from deep in her throat, but the moaning was not one of pain. Her almost-silent moans rose to a crescendo and her body jerked spasmodically for several minutes before the rising of her scream cut off abruptly and she started sighing. Her tense body grew limp as her sighs trailed off to silence.

Longarm had been responding to Phoebe's climax in the best way he'd learned, holding himself buried as deeply as possible while her body writhed and jerked in her consummation. Now he went back to his steady stroking and only a few moments passed before Phoebe's lax limpness gave way to stirring and her body began to grow tense. She started responding to Longarm's thrusts by bringing her hips up to meet them. Her movements were no longer involuntary, but they lost none of the frenzied abandon she'd shown earlier.

"How much longer can you keep going, Longarm?" she asked, gasping as she spoke while keeping her eyes fixed on his face.

"A while. Why? You want me to quit?"

"That's the last thing I'm thinking of! I want you to stay inside me as long as you can!"

"Don't worry about that, Phoebe," he assured her. "I ain't in a hurry no more than you are."

Soon Phoebe began to react once more to Longarm's plunging drives. Now he felt himself sharing her response. The warmth of her body had brought out the aroma of her perfume, and by the time she began the spastic jerking that signaled her consummation Longarm was ready to join her.

As Phoebe's sighs and small cries grew to one ecstatic ululation from deep in her throat, Longarm drove faster and with still more vigor. He maintained his deep steady penetrations until her soft writhing body began trembling and convulsing and he could feel himself beginning his final spasm. Phoebe cried out loudly, as though signaling to him.

Longarm plunged deeper than ever in his climax and held himself pressed against her while he jetted. Phoebe went through her final quick convulsive upthrusts. Then the waves that had been sweeping them began to fade and ebb and they lay quietly. The only noise that now broke the room's silence was the faint susurrus of their gasps in breathing.

Phoebe was the first to speak after they'd lain quietly side by side for several minutes. She asked, "Can you stay with me for a while, Longarm? I don't know about you, but I'd enjoy nothing better than being with you the rest of the day."

"That'd pleasure me too, Phoebe. But I still got a lot of work ahead, and I got a hack waiting for me."

"You don't have to leave right away, do you?"

"Not just this minute. And I ain't real anxious, because what I need to do can wait a while."

"Then I'll have Joseph dismiss the hackney and you can

go back to town in one of my carriages. But put off going as long as you can, because—'' she broke off and sought his lips with hers again.

While they held their kiss, Longarm felt her warm hands slipping along his chest and down his layered muscles until she reached her goal. Under the urgent caresses of her soft busy fingers Longarm soon began to stir and swell.

''There ain't all that big of a hurry,'' he went on when breathlessness forced them to break the kiss. ''The man I got to see next is a nighthawk. The soonest I can figure to get hold of him is after dark. And I ain't leaving Galveston till I close my case here, so we can figure on being together quite a spell.''

When Longarm stepped out of the carriage that Phoebe had insisted on providing to take him back to Galveston's downtown district, the sun was dropping low. So were Longarm's usually high spirits, for when he'd requested the carriageman to swing past the waterfront district, the adobe building with the Barclay's Bank sign had been closed and deserted.

In spite of the day's exertions and his present disappointment, Longarm still felt fresh. He pushed through the batwings of the saloon where he'd cast his bait the night before. The saloon was deserted except for the barkeep who'd been so quick to offer to help him. The man was standing in back of the long stretch of glistening mahogany.

Longarm lifted his hand in a greeting that was also an inquiring gesture. The barkeep nodded, a smile appeared on his face, and he motioned for Longarm to join him. By the time Longarm reached the bar, the man had already set out a glass and a bottle of rye.

Tossing a cartwheel on the bar, Longman poured. He

did not lift the glass at once, but lighted a fresh cigar before saying to the barkeep, "I hope you had some luck doing what you said you'd do last night."

"Maybe so and maybe not," the man replied. "But I think I got a string out that you can pull, if you've a mind to."

"Like I already told you, I ain't learned my way around Galveston yet. If you got a string for me to pull, I'm sure in a hurry to grab hold of it."

"I'll tell you what to do, then," the barkeep said. "When you've had your drink, go outside and walk toward the waterfront till you get to E Street. You can't miss it, and the post office is right in plain sight from the corner where you'll want to turn. There's a hack stand right across from the post office. You ask for Ernie. Tell him Clancey sent you. He'll take care of you from there."

"You mean he'll carry me to where I can find this fellow I'm looking for? Ain't it a bit early? I didn't figure that a man like the one I'm after'd be stirring yet."

"Like I said, Ernie'll take care of you."

"I owe you, anyhow," Longarm told the man. He tossed off his drink and pushed the coin toward the barkeep as he went on, "I'll look in and square accounts with you later on. Right now I'm more concerned about catching up to that fellow you said is waiting for me, because I sure don't wanta miss him."

Leaving the bar, Longarm started walking up the almost deserted street. He reached the corner of E Street and glanced in each direction. Even from a distance he could identify the post office, for in spite of the difference in its architecture from that of the more subdued Federal Building in Denver, it bore the stamp of a government facility.

Turning to follow E Street, he made his way toward the

post office's tall row of gleaming white columns. They were still bright in spite of the gathering dusk, and the street along which he walked was void of pedestrians at the supper hour. He reached the street onto which the post office faced and stopped to look around.

Catercornered across the street a pair of hackney cabs stood on a narrow vacant lot. Longarm turned and started toward them. As he reached the first of the vehicles a man's voice hailed him from the seat atop the carriage.

"You looking for a cab, mister?"

"I reckon I am, but it's got to have a driver named Ernie," Longarm replied. "Leastways, that's the name Clancey gave me."

"And I guess you've got a name?"

"Yep. Custis." As he spoke, Longarm turned his eyes upward, trying to get a clear look at the cabbie, but the man's face was only a shapeless blob of greyish-white in the fast-fading light.

"You've hit the right place, then," the man atop the hack answered. "Climb in and I'll see you get to where you wanta go."

"Where might that be?" Longarm asked.

"There's plenty of time for you to find that out. Just get in and we'll get moving."

Longarm realized fully that he was on the verge of making a target of himself, but in his book that was part of the job he held. He stepped up into the cab. The hackman did not turn to look at him, but slapped the reins on the back of his horse. The cab pulled ahead, and as it passed the plot of ground on which the post office stood Longarm glimpsed a street sign that told him he was on Kemper Street.

"Not that it's going to do you much good to know

where you are, old son," he told himself silently. "It's where you're going that counts. But you sure missed the boat, not getting out and prowling around town today to get acquainted with all its ins and outs. But what you got instead was worth the chance you're taking now."

Trying to make up for his earlier omission, Longarm made every effort to read the street signs that he could see from the cab's interior. The darkness was almost total now, and the cab soon passed beyond the area where streetlights glowed on every corner. It passed through a few intersections where the streets were now shaded in the fast-deepening nighttime gloom, and the corner signs that identified them were impossible to read.

At last the cabbie wheeled his vehicle onto a rutted street lined on both sides with blocky warehouses. The big chunky buildings were unlighted, but that was not important. Longarm realized at once that the buildings on the right-hand side of the street faced the waterfront, and that the cab was taking him to Old Galveston.

With the virtual assurance that he now knew where he was and could easily guess where he was being taken, Longarm relaxed. He took out a cigar and lighted it, letting the fresh vagrant bay breeze that whirled between the big warehouses catch the smoke and trail it in a thin grey line out of the carriage. His cigar was only half consumed when the line of warehouses ended abruptly, and a short distance ahead he could now see the lights of the saloons and the shorefront dwellings reflected in darting flashes from the restless waters of the bay.

Though Longarm expected the hackman to follow the bay shore, the cab took a ruttier road that was between the two rows of houses facing the bay. Now the road was lighted only dimly, and its surface pocked by chuckholes wider and deeper than those on the road which bordered the waterfront. Longarm tossed his cigar butt away and braced himself against the pitching carriage's sudden jolts. He did not relax until the cabman wheeled the vehicle into a dark, high-fenced yard and reined to a stop.

"This is where I was told to bring you," the cabbie said, leaning down from his high seat. "I already been paid, so don't bother digging into your pocket. Just go up to that door yonder and knock and you'll be all right."

"Thanks," Longarm replied as he got out of the cab. "I'll be wanting—"

Before he could finish, the cabbie wheeled his horse and pulled out of the fenced enclosure. Longarm stared at the cab as it vanished.

"Now that's a dead sure giveaway, old son," he muttered under his breath. "You better watch your p's and q's from here on out. Clouter's got you here now, and the way that hackie pulled away, it's a certain-sure sign that he don't intend for you ever to go back."

Settling his holstered Colt in his gun belt, Longarm stepped up to the door and knocked.

Chapter 13

Though Longarm had only half expected that Clouter himself would open the door in response to his knock, he was not prepared to see someone of the hulking size of the man who did open it. After the long ride from town in the darkness of the cab, he was half blinded by the sudden glare and could see the man only in silhouette, but his first glimpse was enough to warn him that trouble might lie ahead.

Outlined against the rectangle of light, the man who'd responded to the knocking stood a good three inches taller than Longarm's own daunting height. He looked as broad as he did tall. His hulking shoulders almost touched each side of the doorjamb, his head looked like a midsummer watermelon, and his upper arms looked like hams from a prize pig. His forearms matched his biceps, and though Longarm could not see his hands clearly, the glimpse he got of them showed thick broad palms and fingers as plump as winter sausages.

"You looking for somebody?" he asked. His voice was another surprise, for it was high pitched and thin.

"I'm supposed to meet a man named Clouter here," Longarm replied.

A grunt was the door-opener's first response, then he said, "You got a name, I guess."

"Sure." Longarm nodded. "Custis."

"Come on in, then," the giant invited, stepping aside.

Longarm had not gotten all the way through the door before his second surprise. As he started to push past the hulking giant, the man wrapped one of his huge arms around Longarm's chest. Though Longarm had been expecting a fracas later, the immediate attack caught him off guard. The big man lifted him as though Longarm's sinewy body was weightless and his huge hand pawed at Longarm's hip until he'd found the butt of his Colt. Longarm felt the weapon being yanked from its holster.

"All right," the giant told Longarm, relaxing his grip. "You can come in the rest of the way now."

Years of poker playing and outfacing enemies stood Longarm to good account. The big man's embracing arm and search had twisted his coat and rumpled it uncomfortably, and Longarm took his time about tugging his shirtsleeves straight and brushing the arms of his coat to smooth the wrinkles. Then he stepped past the giant and surveyed the room. Though he did not like what he saw, he kept his face expressionless.

Clouter was sitting in an armchair at one side of the room. Two more men sat on beer kegs, one on either side of Clouter and a bit in front of him. The hulking giant who'd taken Longarm's Colt was closing the door. Wordlessly, Longarm surveyed the compact panorama.

"It appears like you were sorta expecting me to drop in," he told Clouter calmly.

"I heard that you were poking your nose into things that don't concern you," Clouter told him. "It seemed to me that we'd better have a little talk to clear the air."

"Now, I don't recall that I did anything special," Longarm replied. "Not anything that'd be your affair, anyhow."

"I'd say that killing two of my best men comes under the heading of my affair."

"Why, there's two sides to that story, Clouter. If you look at it from my side, I recall you—"

"Shut up, Custis!" Clouter snapped. He turned to the big man who'd opened the door for Longarm and went on, "Clutch, you stay. And hold on to Custis's gun for the time being. Get over by the door." Sweeping a hand toward the other two he went on, "Red, you and Zamora go in the saloon and have a drink on me. This is going to take a little time. It's too early for us to move anyhow, supposing that we have to."

In silent obedience the two men Clouter had indicated stood up and went through a door in the back wall. Longarm got a brief glimpse of the barroom beyond the opened door, a few men standing in front of the mahogany, their faces reflected in the backbar's wide mirror, and an aproned barkeep filling a glass. While Red and Zamora were entering the bar, the giant Clutch moved as quickly as they did, returning to the entrance door.

Clouter turned back to Longarm. "Now, let's get a few things straight, Custis," he began. "First off, I run things in Galveston. The rich folks on the east side think they do, but when push comes to shove, I'm the boss. You got that?"

"Oh, I got it, all right," Longarm replied. He realized that he was wading in deep water, and knew that he must plunge even deeper. He went on, "I just don't see why you feel like you got to show off about what a big man you are."

Clouter frowned angrily, but his voice was level as he went on, "When I hear about anybody who gets out of line in Galveston by asking questions I don't want answered, I get upset. Fool questions upset applecarts, Custis."

"I've heard folks say that," Longarm said, nodding. "But I don't see what you're so upset about. If I recall rightly, the last time you and me talked you made me an offer that sounded pretty good. You said you had a man that you wanted put outa the way, and I'm the one you offered the job to."

"Now, hold on!" Clouter exclaimed. "Just stop jawing and listen to me."

"If you got something to say, then go ahead and spit it out," Longarm invited. He was feeling a bit of relief now, though he was aware that the ice underfoot was still very thin.

"You killed two of my men instead of just the one I had in mind to get rid of." Clouter's voice was flatly expressionless. "And you did it without me telling you to."

"I ain't agreeing to that," Longarm objected. "Them two fellows came after me. I didn't go looking for them."

"I haven't said you did," Clouter pointed out. His anger seemed to be diminishing. He went on, "I'm going to lay my cards face-up, Custis. You can believe it or not, but I didn't send both of them. I told Sellers to get those bonds away from you, and since he took Sid with him, I've got an idea he was figuring on doing a little business of his own on the side."

Though Longarm realized that he could ease the tension by mentioning the bonds he'd found in the rooming house, he decided to keep quiet about them. He nodded his agreement and stayed silent, waiting for Clouter to go on.

"I'm a big enough man to let bygones be bygones," Clouter continued. "And the only thing I've got against you is killing one of my men that I didn't have any reason to get rid of."

"All I did was shoot back. I didn't jump him. Him and the other fellow along with him jumped me."

166

"I don't guess I can blame you for that. But you made another mistake, asking all those questions about me in town."

To keep his cover intact, Longarm retorted quickly, "You told me you wanted a job done. I done it, then started out to find you and get my pay. Sure as God made little green apples, there ain't no way I know of to find a man without asking about him."

"I can't argue against that. But I work best when nobody knows too much about me."

"Soon as I mentioned your name to that barkeep downtown, he knew you and didn't make no bones about telling me," Longarm pointed out.

"He's one of my men," Clouter admitted. "And I've got a few more where it counts. But that's not here nor there. Since you've found out how things work here in Galveston, do you still want to work for me?"

"Why, that depends," Longarm said slowly and thoughtfully. Then, keeping to the role he'd undertaken, he asked, "First off, I'd want you to say what's in it for me."

"Plenty, if you're the man I take you for. I've got a lot of strings out, Custis, and every time I pull one it means money. Usually a lot of money."

"Money talks. Talking about money don't make nobody rich."

"What would you say to—" Clouter stopped when the door into the saloon opened and the man called Red slipped into the room. Clouter looked at him with a frown.

"What the hell do you mean busting in on me?" he asked.

"I'm sorry, but I had to, boss," Red replied. "I got something to tell you in private."

"Well, spit it out."

167

Red looked at Longarm as he said, "I better tell you without nobody else listening."

"All right, if it's that private," Clouter said, "come on. We'll step across the room."

Being careful not to display too much interest, Longarm watched as Clouter led his man to the furthest corner of the room. Their heads close together, they held a brief whispered conversation. Though Longarm thought the two men were talking for an unduly long time, he was careful not to appear too interested in them. His only movement was to take out a fresh cigar and light it.

At last Clouter and Red finished their talk. Clouter headed for the chair he'd been occupying and settled back into it while Red crossed over to the door and began whispering to Clutch. The giant had to bend forward to bring his ear near Red's mouth. He listened for a moment, then nodded. Red started back toward the door of the saloon and was halfway across the room when he stopped suddenly and turned back to the giant at the door.

"C'mere, Clutch!" he called. "I forgot part of what I was supposed to tell you."

Clutch lumbered forward, heading for Red. His course took him behind the chair in which Longarm was sitting. Longarm had returned his attention to Clouter. When the giant stopped unexpectedly and clamped his arms around both Longarm and the chair, pinning him in a sitting position, Longarm was taken completely by surprise. His muscles tensed in lightning-swift reaction, but it was too late.

"See that you hang on to him," Clouter told his henchman.

"Don't worry, boss. I got him good," Clutch replied.

Clouter had not moved during the brief episode. He

looked at Longarm now, his eyes cold, and said, "If you don't want Clutch to pull you into little pieces, you'll keep your damned mouth shut. If Red's wrong, you've got nothing to worry about. If he's right—well, that's something I'll settle real fast."

Longarm had seen enough of Clouter to know that the outlaw boss meant exactly what he said. He nodded, but did not speak.

"All right, Red," Clouter went on. "Go get that fellow you told me about and bring him back here."

Red nodded and started for the door leading into the barroom. He returned in a moment, accompanied by a frowsty thin-faced man. Not only did he need a shave, he also needed clothes to replace the torn and travel-stained garments he had on.

Longarm kept a poker face as he looked at the new arrival, but he'd known from the moment the man entered that he was on the thinnest ice he'd been on for a long time. He'd recognized the newcomer with the first glimpse he'd gotten of his face. The man was Pleas Retter, a petty sneak thief who'd tried unsuccessfully to graduate to robbing a U.S. mail coach. Longarm had tracked him down, arrested him, testified at his trial, and escorted him to the federal prison.

"Here's the fellow I was telling you about, boss," Red said to Clouter.

Without rising from his chair, Clouter shifted around to look at Retter and said, "Red says you know this fellow sitting in front of me. He says his name's Custis. Is that right?"

"No. It ain't but half right, mister," Retter answered promptly. "His first name's Custis, all right, but his last name's Long. He's the U. S. marshal that folks calls Longarm."

"You're sure?" Clouter asked.

"Damn right I am! Hell, he chased me down and taken me in after a job I pulled up in Colorado and I seen him plenty of times after that, in court and all. He's Longarm, for sure!"

"That's all I need to know." Clouter nodded. "Now you go on back in the barroom with Red." He turned to Red and went on, "Tell the barkeep that whatever this fellow wants to drink is on the house."

"You mean all I'm going to get is a drink or two?" Retter demanded.

"You'll get a lot more than a drink," Clouter replied. "You've done me a big favor and I expect to pay you for it. I don't know what Red promised you, but I'll take care of you all right, as soon as I get through with my business in here."

Even before Red closed the door into the saloon, Clouter was turning back to Longarm. "You've ripped a hole in your britches this time," he said. "I never was quite easy about all the palaver you passed out. It didn't sound wrong, but it didn't sound just right, either. Now, do you feel like telling me why you're really here, or will I have to get Clutch to beat it out of you?"

"You might as well save your breath, Clouter," Longarm replied. His voice held no hint of fear or worry, nor was his tone boastful. "I been in worse fixes than this with a lot better men up against me than you'll ever be, and nobody's ever made me say anything yet that I didn't want to."

For a moment Clouter stared at Longarm, then he nodded slowly and said, "I guess you're right about that. I can tell a tough man when I run across one. But I suppose you know what the only other answer is."

170

"Oh, I'd imagine you feel like you'll have to kill me," Longarm replied. His tone was still casual and unworried. "And better men than you've tried that, too, but I'm still on my own two feet and aim to walk away from Galveston on 'em."

"Nobody walks away from Galveston Island, they've got to—" Clouter began. He stopped short, and an evil grin rippled across his lips. Then he said, "But what you just said gives me an idea." He turned to Clutch and went on, "Go in the barroom, tell Red and Zamora to come in here."

"You want the other fellow, too? The one that snitched?" Clutch asked.

"No, just our own—" Clouter stopped short, then went on, "You just gave me another idea. Sure, tell the boys to bring the snitcher along with them."

Clutch nodded and went through the door to the barroom. He returned in a moment, followed by the three other outlaws.

"Zamora, is the big boat down at the dock?" Clouter asked.

"Sure, boss, just like always," the outlaw said.

"Then you hurry down there and bring back some rope," Clouter went on. "Small, tough rope. I want it to tie this Longarm up good before we start out."

"Wait a minute!" Retter broke in. "When this fellow said I was to come along with him, I figured you was ready to pay me. Now you start talking about taking a boat ride. I don't—"

"Don't worry," Clouter told him. "This place here isn't as good a hideout as the one we're going to. And don't worry about getting paid off. I'm going to take care of you."

171

"Well, I guess it's all right, then," Retter agreed. "I sure don't aim to be cut out, after I done you a big favor."

For a moment Longarm felt a small tremor of something akin to fear, but he did not allow it to show on his face. Then he clenched his teeth and turned his mind to planning a way of escaping from the outlaws. He still had not found a workable scheme by the time Zamora returned with a coil of small rope.

"You tie Longarm up," Clouter told his henchman. "And do a good job, because from what little I've heard about him on the grapevine, he's trickier than hell. Just don't tie his feet. He's a big fellow, and I don't want to risk drawing any notice by carrying him when we go outside."

"Don't worry, boss man," Zamora replied. "I been a sailor since I was a *bambino*. He don't get away when I tie him up."

Dropping to his knees behind Longarm, Zamora pulled Longarm's hands behind his back and began twisting and knotting the thin rope around his wrists.

Longarm had already decided that the odds against him were too great and the place they were in too confined to make an effort to get away worthwhile. Without his Colt and with Clouter and the other two outlaws standing watching, there was little or no chance for any effort he might make to succeed. He stood without resisting while Zamora lashed his wrists together and knotted the rope, pulling it so painfully tight that Longarm could feel the strands cutting into his flesh.

"He's ready, boss," Zamora reported at last as he gave the ends of the rope a final tug before standing up. "He's not going to bother nobody now. But what we do with him?"

"We march him down to the boat," Clouter replied. "Clutch, you go first and wrestle it away from the dock. Move it along the shore till it's right by this place here and we don't have too far to walk. I wouldn't want anybody to see us and start wondering what was going on."

"How about just paying me off and letting me go about my business?" Retter suggested again. "I don't like boats one little bit. I'd be glad to take whatever—"

"Quit bellyaching, damn it!" Clouter snapped. Turning to face the scrawny outlaw he went on, "I haven't got enough cash on me to pay you what you did is worth. Now, if you want a bunch of double-eagles jingling in your pocket, you'll do what I say and keep your mouth closed till I ask you a question."

Retter gulped and pressed his lips together into a thin line, but he made no reply. He fell in beside Red as Clouter led the way outside and the little group moved away from the saloon and headed across the sandy beach to the water's edge.

Longarm had maintained his silence since the odds had gone against him so suddenly. He broke it now.

"Mind telling me where you aim to take me?" he asked Clouter.

"You'll find out fast enough," Clouter replied. "And it wouldn't make much difference to you. You haven't been on the island here long enough to know, and there's not anything you can do to stop me from taking you anywhere I choose."

They reached the shore a few moments later. A small single-masted fishing boat, its sail furled, had been pulled up to a narrow two-plank wide pier that extended a dozen feet into the water. The vessel was only a bit larger than the fishing boat in which Tom Saunders had brought Longarm to Galveston.

"All right," Clouter said, "Red, you and Clutch get Long aboard first. Then the rest of us can get on. Zamora, you give us a push off the wharf, since you're the sailor of the bunch."

There was a moment of half-organized confusion as the men boarded, then Zamora pulled the mooring rope free and pushed the boat away from shore. He scrambled aboard and stepped to the mast to raise the sail. The triangular canvas billowed out, and the boat began moving slowly forward.

"You better tell me where we going, boss," Zamora said.

"You know the water better than I do," Clouter replied. "Just take us where the sharks are thickest."

Chapter 14

Clouter's remark was not needed to remind Longarm of his precarious position, but he gave no sign of even having heard the gang leader's comment. He asked no questions and did not resist when Clutch shoved him down on the bottom of the boat and stood towering above him.

Longarm squirmed around for a moment, trying to find a more comfortable position on the sloping boards of the boat's bottom and let his muscles relax. He watched the small flurry of activity on the boat as Clouter's men distributed themselves in the vessel and the sail was raised. The wind was blowing gently across Galveston Island from the Gulf of Mexico, and the crowded little craft made slow headway as it it tacked in its zigzag course, pushing across the night-black water.

There were lights visible on Galveston Island, but all of them were distant from the shore. The houses along the waterfront seemed deserted and there were no other boats in the water. The black night offered Longarm no encouragement.

As the boat started veering away from the shore, Longarm saw one or two dim glints high in the dark sky from the deep-water side of Pelican Island. For a moment he thought there might be a chance for an encounter with another vessel, which could offer him an opportunity to escape, then he realized that they were the masthead lights of a tall ship putting out to sea.

They passed the high bulky warehouses that faced the waterfront, but the big buildings were all dark. A few lights from the city brightened the sky beyond them, but after they'd sailed past Galveston's boundaries, blackness took over ahead of the small boat and only the faint gleam of starshine dotted the ink-dark surface of the water.

"I guess you know where you're going, Zamora?" Clouter asked as the boat continued its slow but steadily relentless progress through the gloom.

"Sure, boss," the helmsman answered. "You said you want to go where is the most sharks. We got to be closer to deep water, like is in gulf. Is always sharks there."

"We'll give 'em a good meal, then," Clouter said.

"You mean you're going to toss Longarm overboard?" Red asked. His voice was subdued, lacking its usual gruffness.

"Can you come up with a better way to get rid of him?" Clouter's voice was calm as he threw back the question.

"I guess you'll shoot him first?"

"Why waste a bullet?" Clouter countered. "He'll be shark bait two minutes after he hits the water."

"Well . . ." Red hesitated a moment, then went on, "It just seems to me he oughta be dead first. Tossing him in alive is a sorta mean thing to do. Being eaten up by a bunch of sharks while you still know what's happening to you ain't like taking a bullet."

"Of course not," Clouter answered. "But it saves us having to cart him away out of town and dig a grave along the beach."

"That ain't much of a chore," Red said. "Longarm wouldn't be the first one you've had us bury."

"Granting that," Clouter told his man, "even when you bury a man you've shot there's always a risk of some nosy son of a bitch digging up his body."

"I don't recall that ever happening to us," Red said.

"Longarm's a different kind of case, Red. Remember, he's a federal man."

"What difference does that make? In my book a lawman's a lawman," Red replied.

"A lot," Clouter answered. 'When he doesn't show up or send in a report, Longarm's boss is going to start asking questions. It's likely he'll even send somebody looking for him."

"That hadn't occurred to me," Red admitted. His voice was thoughtful.

Clouter went on, "The first thing you know, we'd have a whole damn swarm of U.S. marshals trying to find him, and Galveston Island's not all that big. How long do you think it'd take those fellows to find a grave along the beach? Why do you think that I had you drop that Secret Service Agent in the gulf?"

"I see what you're getting at," Red said. "It still seems like a sorta mean thing to do, but I got to admit it makes sense to do it."

Lying in the bottom of the boat, Longarm had listened to the exchange between Clouter and Red. Fear was not part of his makeup, though thoughts of the fate Clouter had planned for him raised Longarm's hackles. He began working harder at trying to force some slack into the rope that bound his wrists behind him, but Zamora had done his job well. There was not even a hair's breadth of slack in the binding.

Squirming around in his efforts to break free started Longarm sliding along the boat's sloping bottom planks. The slipping had been so slow and his downward slide so

177

gradual that the first awareness of his movements came to him when he felt the chill of cold bilge water seeping through the seat of his trousers. He worked his fingers as best he could along the wet fabric, and they were suddenly cold and wet as they reached the two or three inches of water that sloshed gently along the boat's bottom.

When his hands felt the water's chill Longarm bent his elbows instinctively, spreading them away from his ribs to get his arms apart. Rolling to lie on his side had lifted his hands out of the bilge water. He rubbed them together as best he could, trying to dry them and rid them of the clinging greasy scum that now coated them.

Longarm's hands were not only soaked with water now. They were filmed, coated with the scum of oily liquid that had accumulated on the surface of the two or three inches of water he'd plunged them into. As he worked his fingers, rubbing them together to get rid of the clinging goo, Longarm suddenly realized that he might have stumbled on the one chance he had to break free. He flexed his knees and pushed as he wriggled down the sloping bottom of the boat until his hands and wrists were submerged again.

Holding himself in the cramped and uncomfortable position he'd now gotten into on the boat's sloping bottom, Longarm started trying to lever his wrists and twist them to bring his hands together. After several futile efforts he could feel the lashing going slack.

Though the motions he was making were painful, he was encouraged now by the knowledge that the cold, semi-liquid greasy gunk along the keel was working on his bonds. He was just beginning to feel that he was making progress when Zamora's voice broke the silence.

"We are where the sharks come, boss," he said. "You want I should throw out anchor?"

"Hell, there's no use to anchor," Clouter told him.

"You and Red just drop the sail. I want to get away from here quick when our job's done. You know how it is with the fishing boats, and they're likely to put out any time of the day or night to catch a tide turn."

From the bottom of the boat Longarm could see the four men along the rail as silhouettes against the night sky. Without slackening his attention to the bonds he was soaking in the bilge water he began watching them.

Clouter raised his voice again. "Clutch! Go ahead now and do what I told you to!"

Longarm saw the giant moving along the side of the boat, then he forgot to keep working his wrists as Clutch edged along the thwart of the boat and reached Retter. Suddenly he grabbed Retter and lifted him bodily, then tossed him into the water.

"What in hell?" Red exclaimed as Retter's startled shout ended in a splash that sent spray dashing over the fishing boat.

"I want a lot of sharks here," Clouter broke in. His voice was colder than the water that splashed over the men in the boat. "When you want sharks to get together you've got to give 'em some bait."

Longarm redoubled his efforts. More of the greasy bilge water had seeped into the rope by now. He succeeded in rotating his wrists in spite of the tightly lashed strands that bound them together.

A scream ending in a gurgle sounded from the water's surface and Clutch exclaimed, "A shark's got Retter!"

As the sound of Retter's last scream and the noises of splashing water died away, Longarm curled the fingers and palm of one hand into the tightest cone he could form and began trying to pull one hand free from the loops of rope encircling his wrists. He moved more confidently now, heedless of the small noises he might make, for the sounds

179

of disturbed water had begun again, telling him that the maneaters were gathering.

"We'll wait for a few more sharks," Clouter told his men. "There's a dozen or so down there now, and the blood in the water will have fifty more here inside of a few minutes. Then we'll take care of Longarm."

Longarm's hands and fingers were slick with oily bilge water by now and the rope that bound them was even slicker. Slowly and grudgingly the hand he was trying to pull out of the circling rope began slipping through the bindings.

Suddenly it popped loose, and his wrist and hand came free. The suddenly slackened rope slid off his other wrist and dropped with a small splash into the thin oil-streaked line of water that sloshed along the boat's keel. Longarm sat up and began rubbing his wrists and hands to get the numbness out of his fingers.

Old son, he told himself silently as he slid his hand under his belt buckle to grasp the curved butt of his derringer, *you got to do a mite of scheming to get this mess worked out right. There's four men besides you in this boat, and you only get two shots outa this derringer. You better come up with some kinda scheme that'll level out the odds.*

Thumbing back the derringer's hammer to full cock, Longarm slowly stood up. The four renegades were lined up along the side of the boat, their attention on the black swirling water. They were paying no attention to Longarm. All of them—Zamora near the stern, Red next to him, then Clouter and the massive Clutch—were staring down at the bubbled froth floating on the black water.

Longarm hesitated for a moment. Shooting a man in the back, even an outlaw or renegade, was an idea alien to his creed. He was saved the repugnant thought of a back-shot when Clutch turned to say something to Clouter. From the corners of his eyes the giant caught a glimpse of movement when Longarm brought up his derringer.

"Look out!" Clutch yelled.

Longarm's Colt, which Clutch had taken earlier, was still protruding from the giant's belt. Clutch grabbed for it, but he was not fast enough. He had the butt of the Colt in his huge pawlike hand when Longarm triggered the derringer.

Even the massive bulk of the giant Clutch was not great enough to withstand the impact of the soft heavy .44 caliber chunk of lead that flew from the derringer. The bullet smashed into Clutch's broad chest and destroyed his precarious balance.

Clutch's knees were just below the wide sturdy timber that circled the little boat's rim and served as a rail. The impact of Longarm's bullet started him toppling toward the water, and when Clutch felt himself falling he grabbed with both hands for the rail.

When he opened his right hand and clamped it on the wide rail, the swell of Clutch's oversized fingers expanded and locked the Colt's trigger guard to his trigger finger, but the giant was able to hold on with both hands in spite of the impediment. His grip did not stop his fall, but did keep him from becoming instant shark meat. He toppled into the water and dangled half in, half out of it, held up by his massive hands, which were still clinging to the rail.

Clouter had started to turn around when Clutch shouted, as had Red and Zamora. As Clouter turned he'd been reaching for the pistol in his shoulder holster. He had it out and was bringing it down to fire when Red started toward Longarm.

Red had drawn his revolver at almost the same time Clouter had, and was raising it from his hip. He stepped in

181

front of Clouter just as the underworld boss triggered off the shot intended for Longarm. The bullet smashed into Red instead of whistling to its intended target.

Red's body jerked when the bullet slammed into him. He lurched forward, turning and stumbling. He began waving his arms involuntarily as he tried to regain his balance. In his struggle to stay on his feet he tightened his trigger finger.

By one of fate's unfathomable quirks, Red's revolver was in line with his boss when the shot was finally triggered. The bullet took Clouter in the cheekbone and its impact was great enough to send the gang leader toppling. His knees buckled as he sagged backward, and though he was in his final throes his outstretched arms were waving wildly.

Clouter's left hand slapped against Red's shirt and locked into its fabric with all the strength that was in his dying grip. The impact of his hand against Red was not enough to slow or to change his body's backward fall. Clouter kept toppling toward the water, dragging the dying Red with him. Both their bodies sagged across the boat's low rail. Longarm got only a passing glimpse of the dead men's legs and feet sliding downward, then they vanished below the rail and disappeared under the surface of the water.

Zamora did not wear a gun belt. His weapon was the knife. He'd pulled it from its belt sheath when Clutch's warning cry broke the night's stillness and started toward Longarm.

Longarm had been gazing in astonishment at his enemies toppling like dominoes, but the mirrorlike flashing of the knife blade caught his eye as Zamora darted forward. Swiveling with the speed and agility that were almost instinctive after so many battles with the lawless, Longarm fired the derringer's second barrel. The bullet smashed into Zamora's chest and started him whirling like a clumsy man-sized top.

Still impelled toward Longarm, Zamora fought to keep on his forward course, but the speed with which he was moving proved to be his undoing. His whirls and the sudden lurching of the boat as the bodies of Clouter and Zamora vanished into the water propelled him away from Longarm, to the boat's gunwales, and he fell to join his companions in the dark water.

Though Longarm was a veteran of many deadly encounters, he couldn't remember being in a closer brush with death nor ever before seeing so many deadly antagonists sign their own death warrants in such a short span of time. His forefinger was still tightly closed around the stubby derringer's trigger when he turned to look along the line of the boat's gunwales.

To Longarm's surprise, Clutch's big hands were still locked on the gunwales and Longarm's Colt was still dangling from the giant's forefinger. Longarm pocketed his derringer before stepping up to the rail. He peered over the side of the boat and saw that Clutch's head was drooping, his face below the surface of the water.

Longarm began prying Clutch's forefinger, which was still passed through the Colt's trigger guard. At last he suceeded in loosening the locked finger and sliding his Colt free. He wiped the weapon on his trouser leg and restored it to its holster before returning to the unpleasant job of freeing the dead man's hands. He was still working at it when from the black depths the tapering nose of a shark broke the surface. The big fish's sandpapery skin rasped Longarm's hands as the shark's leap carried it out of the water and across the deck until its curved mouth was resting on the boat's thwarts.

Out of its element and struggling to return to it, the shark began squirming, lashing its tail in the water while its long pointed snout broke the surface on the opposite side of the small craft. The little boat keeled to one side, then to the other as the shark arched and wriggled in its struggle to return to the water's depths.

Clinging to the sail's boom with one hand, Longarm slid out his Colt and emptied its cylinder into the big fish's struggling body, five shots in quick succession. He was well aware that his time to work was sharply limited, for the small boat was shipping water each time it heeled, and the night-black waters of the bay reflected the stars in a rippling mirror, broken by the fins of other sharks attracted by the stranded fish's antics.

Longarm tried to puzzle out a way of reloading his Colt with only one hand free, but could think of none that would be practical in his present precarious situation. Even with his limited seafaring knowledge he was keenly aware that the shark's frenzied thrashing could easily overturn the small fishing boat or sink it. He did not allow his mind to dwell on what would happen to him once he was in the water.

A woman's voice, faint above the splashing, reached his ears. It sounded surprisingly close. Longarm looked out over the wide expanse of black water, and for the first time saw the prow of another boat. It was still some distance away, and the glow of starshine reflected from the disturbed surface of the sea was dim, but the boat was close enough now for him to see and recognize Topacia Trechas.

"I will kill the shark," she called. "Hold tight! Once it dies, I can pull close enough for you to jump in my boat!"

Longarm had no choice. He took a firm grip on the sail boom and waited. Topacia moved into the prow of her small boat as it drew closer and picked up something from the deck. As the boat got still closer Longarm recognized the weapon in Topacia's hand as a sawed-off shotgun.

She leaned across the rail of her boat, paying no attention to the swaying, weaving head and fearsome teeth of the big shark, and shoved the muzzle of the shotgun against its head. The report when she pulled the trigger was muffled, but the shark's flat head seemed to explode as the gun boomed. The shark quivered and then threshed into its prolonged dying spasm that rocked and tilted the boat Longarm was in, then the big fish was motionless.

Longarm recognized the urgency in Topacia's voice when she called, "Hurry! Get into my boat! Yours is sinking!"

Longarm glanced around and now he could see that the stern of the vessel was already under water, and he clung to the boom only long enough to holster his Colt before taking the two or three precarious steps across the slanting deck and leaping into Topacia's boat.

She pushed off at once, sending her boat backward with all her strength. The span of black water between her craft and the sinking boat that Longarm had just left widened swiftly. There was enough distance between the two small vessels for Topacia's boat to escape the undertow when the outlaw's vessel suddenly reared until its bowsprit pointed to the night sky.

It stood poised for a few seconds, then plunged down and disappeared under the black water. The sea's surface boiled and bubbled for a few minutes before it grew smoothly placid once more. All that remained of the vanished vessel was a litter of debris floating on the surface.

"I reckon you saved my bacon that time," Longarm told his rescuer. "I seen enough men gobbled up by sharks tonight, and I sure thought for a minute or so that I was going to be shark bait myself. But how in tunket did you know where I was?''

"I did not know," she replied. As she spoke, Topacia was lighting a ship's lantern that hung from the rigging. "I started out to fish, then I heard shooting and went to find why.''

"Well, I'm sure obliged," Longarm told her. He pulled out one of his long thin cigars and started to light it before he realized that not only was the cigar too wet, but that his clothing was also soaked and dripping. Tossing the cigar into the water he went on, "Now, I ain't in no hurry to get back to Galveston, so if you want to do what you came out here for, I'll go along with you while you fish.''

Topacia shook her head. "It's no use to fish now. When too many sharks are in the water, fish won't come around.'' She was looking closely at Longarm in the lantern light. "I have a *cabina* on Pelican Island, and it's closer than going home. We'll put to shore and I'll make a fire, and you can get dry and warm.''

"Don't put yourself out none on my account," Longarm said. "I ain't made outa sugar, I won't melt before I dry off.''

Topacia was already changing course. "No," she told him. "It's not good to stay on the water. We will be better in my *cabina*.''

"You sure were right when you said we'd be better off in this cabin of yours than out on that cold black water," Longarm said.

Wearing only his damp long johns, he was standing close to the small stove in Topacia's cabin. The cabin was small, its furnishings only the stove, a bed and a chair. A clothesline stretched across one end of the cabin held

Longarm's outer garments. A thin line of steam was beginning to rise from a bucket of water on the stove. Topacia stepped past Longarm and lifted the bucket to the floor.

"I'll bathe you now, so you can get warm," she told Longarm. She stepped up to him and began unbuttoning the long johns.

"Now, hold on!" Longarm protested. "We don't know each other hardly at all, Topacia!"

"But we will," she promised. By now she had unbuttoned the undergarment to Longarm's waist. Before Longarm could grasp her busy hands Topacia pulled the long johns to his thighs and let them slide on down to his ankles. "*Almirante!*" she smiled. "In my country we have a saying, Longarm, *Quanto antes melhor*. It means sooner is better than later. Come with me."

While she spoke, Topacia was unbuttoning her dress. With her free hand she grasped Longarm and let the dress fall to the floor as she led him to the waiting bed.

Watch for

LONGARM AND THE HANGMAN'S LIST

one hundred thirtieth novel in
the bold LONGARM series
from Jove

coming in October!